PUZZLED

By

Donna Sako

Dedication

To my Writers Group for their support.

Copy write & disclaimer

This is a work of fiction. Names, characters, businesses, places, events and incidents are either the products of the author's imagination or used in a fictitious manner. Any resemblance to actual persons, living or dead, or actual events is purely coincidental.

Table of Contents

Chapter One: The Beginning

Pumping and beeping of the medical equipment were heard throughout the room.

"Scalpel", the surgeon said as he was viewing the body before him. Slowly he began to make an incision and then pulled back the tissue. "Oh, My. Do you see what I see?"

The attending physician peered into the body. "Yes, I do." he replied. "I've never seen one before have you?"

"No. Now I have to tell him. That will not be easy."

After the surgery the patient was wheeled into the one of the recovery rooms and attached to monitoring machines and given oxygen.

Nurses, doctors came and went for several hours checking on the patient. But he lay quietly without movement. No one was awaiting the man's status. The room was empty and silent except for the machines.

Later that evening, Jim, the patient, was beginning to awaken. His eye lids fluttered a bit as they opened. His eyesight was blurred at first and he felt the oxygen mask upon his face. As his sight became clearer he also heard the pumping and beeping within the room. "Where am I?" he thought. "How did I get here?" The last thing he remembered was driving his car to work. "Was I in an accident?"

A nurse who was walking past his room suddenly saw that Jim was awake. She stopped and entered the room. "Glad to see you're awake." She reached for the clipboard at the end of the bed and made some notes as she read the readings on the machines. "I will let the doctor know you're awake. He will want to give you an update on your status." The nurse replaced the clipboard, turned and walked out the door.

Jim quietly remained in his bed feeling some discomforting pain, puzzled, tired and sluggish. A Few minutes passed and then his doctor knocked on the entrance. "Hello, Jim, I am Doctor Morris." Once he got Jim's attention, he entered the room and closed the opened door behind him.

The doctor pulled a chair from the far side of the room and placed it next to Jim and then lifted the clipboard from the lower bed and sat in the chair. "Jim, I've been going over your stats and you are doing just fine. You have two broken ribs but they will heal in about 2 months. You had some internal bleeding as well which we corrected in surgery. You should be able to go home. As long as your work is not physical, you can also go back to work."

Jim, moved to remove his mask. "Sorry, Jim. Let me help you. You might need to still have the oxygen so if you feel faint let me know."

"What happened to me?" Jim asked.

"Well, there was a car accident. You were hit by another car which ran a red light. The air bag is what caused the ribs to break. One of the broken ribs caused some internal bleeding which is now corrected. The police are still investigating the accident, so I do not have much to tell you about that. But I did need to inform you of your injuries."

Jim listened as the doctor continued. "As I said we did surgery for some cracked ribs and bleeding. They will heal fine. But there is something else we found. The doctor paused and took a deep breath before he spoke. "Do you remember over 50 years ago in 2020 when the climate change was playing havoc with the world?" Jim nodded wondering what that had to do with him. "Well, the public was never told this because the governments of the world were afraid of the repercussions." The doctor then reached inside his inside coat pocket and pulled out a piece of paper and handed it to Jim. "Thus before I can reveal what I must, you must sign this form stating that you will never expose what I am about to tell you without approval from the government or only to your doctor if you become sick or injured."

Shocked, Jim defiantly looked into the doctor's eyes, "And if I refuse to sign it?"

"Well then, I cannot tell you what I really need to tell you. You see, I must give you the option. Government requires it."

"Just how important is it?"

"Pretty important. You will probably want to know it." The doctor offered Jim the pen and clipboard. "You can use this to sign it."

Pondering the entire situation, Jim reached for the pen and after reading the form, he glanced at the doctor and signed it.

"Thank you, Jim," the doctor said as he took the pen and clipboard, removed the form and replaced it in his inside pocket of his white coat. "I can't give you a copy or leave it with your hospital information because no one, not even the staff, should be aware of this. This is between you, me and the government. "

The doctor moved closer to Jim and began to whisper, "When the earth was in danger of losing humans, the governments began to take steps to insure that...some humans would be strong enough to survive. To do so, they did gene manipulation. They created stronger genes by creating artificial ones to combine with our human genes. What I mean to say is.....you're not fully human. You are.....partially robotic."

Jim was horrified. "But I bleed. I feel. I love. I hate. How can I be robotic? I am not a machine!"

"I know this is hard to digest. But you have the markers inside you. We saw them when we did the surgery. And yes, you do all those things but you are also robotic. You need to be aware of this in case you need health treatments later. We still do not know how this will affect you. They did not have time to do trials before creating you and others."

"How will this affect me if I want to have children? Can I have children? What will they be?"

"Jim, I have been told that you were created to have children and be able to mate with both other robots as well as full humans."

"How many of US are there? What are the telling signs? Can I meet them?"

"I do not know how many, I do not know the signs other than the ones inside you, and there is not a log I can refer you to. The government is the only one who knows, other than the doctor who has found you, and only the government knows, if we tell them. So the list, so to speak, is not counting every one of the robots. How the government keeps and tracks the information, I do not know. I do not think they will tell you either, since they want this to be kept quiet. They fear that people will once again create the wars of the past if they knew. They want humans to survive ...which is why they created the robots. They feared extinction if they did not create people like you."

Feeling faint from the news and the need for his oxygen mask, Jim motioned for the mask to be returned. The doctor arose replacing the mask on Jim's face. After moving his chair and the clipboard back to its original spot, the doctor left the room closing the door behind him. Jim closed his eyes praying this was a bad dream.

Chapter Two: The Mystery Begins

Dr. Morris closed the door behind him as he left Jim's room and slowly made his way to his office which was on same floor but on the other side of the hospital. Reaching the office door, he placed his hand over the entrance ID key near the door handle. After a brief flash of light from the ID key, the door clicked allowing him to turn the handle and enter his office. As he entered the ceiling light turned on allowing him enter safely. Dr. Morris closed the door which automatically locked behind him.

The room contained two floor to ceiling book cases, a desk and chair with a computer, a phone device, and other normal office fixtures. There were at least 3 other side chairs and a sofa mid room with a TV on the wall. In the middle between them was a circle in the floor. In front of his desk was a small two person sofa reserved for visitor consultations.

He gazed about the room and then made his way to his desk. The signed document from Jim was removed from his coat pocket. Dr. Morris gazed at the document and then reached for his phone device. Without lifting the private conversation handle he spoke, "Alexa, call the Federal Bureau of Health."

He listened patiently while ringing was heard in the otherwise quiet room. "Federal Bureau of Health, how may I help you?"

"Would like to report a Robot."

"Thank you. I will connect you to Dr. Sherlock."

"Hello, Dr. Sherlock, How may I help you?"

"Dr. Sherlock, this is Dr. Dwayne Morris of Baltimore, Maryland. I have a Robot to report."

"Fantastic. Let me turn on my enhancer." With that remark a hologram of Dr. Sherlock appeared within the room over the three foot circle on the floor just mid room. "Please activate your enhancer as well."

Dr. Morris pushed a button on the phone device so his image was also seen by Dr. Sherlock on his circle.

"Did everything go well?"

"Yes, I think." Dr. Morris hesitated. "Why must we call them Robots?"

"Because it is the only way we can try and control them."

"But have you ever thought of the physiological damage of using that term?"

"Yes, but without that fear, they would tell the world. We cannot let that happen."

"I'm sorry but I think it is wrong. Why not just tell them the truth?"

"We will tell them but only when we are sure they are ready. If they knew... there may be another uprising and that could upset the balance we have finally created."

"You know, balance, is rarely permanent. We could be making it worse."

"That is not for us to choose. Our Governments must decide."

Dr. Morris walked to the circle and handed the document to the image before him.

"Thank you for getting this. We will place it in a file here and begin to track him." Dr. Sherlock looked closely at the document. "We need to see how he progressed."

The visual link and conversation were suddenly ended.

Chapter Three: Marie

Marie was working in her office on her computer in the 20 story office building overlooking the Chesapeake Bay. She took a moment to stop typing and gaze outside through the floor to ceiling glass window that was beside her on one side of the room. She could see sea gulls flying above and feeding below as they dove to catch fish near the surface and then soared skyward and then toward the marshes where she suspected their nests were located.

Her office was much like everyone's. A desk, chair and extra chairs for visitors as well as book shelves filled with books and other items. A large file cabinet was off in a corner of the room. Amid the room was the 3 foot circle for her enhancer.

As she returned to her typing, her phone rang. Feeling a bit annoyed she commanded, "Alexa, answer."

"Marie Gloss, How may I help you?"

"Marie, glad to catch you! This is Dr. Michael Sherlock of the FBH. We have an assignment for you." With that statement a hologram appeared in the circle containing Dr. Sherlock. "Jim Boggs was undergoing surgery and the attending physician, Dr. Dwayne Morris, found a marker of a robot. I would like you to infiltrate and report findings."

Marie pushed her enhancer button on her phone which allowed her hologram to appear in Dr. Sherlock's office. "I will assume you have the paperwork?"

"Yes."

Marie reached into the circle and took a document from Dr. Sherlock's hand.

"It is a copy of the original form and our paper request for investigation."

Reading the forms as Dr. Sherlock waited for her approval, Marie was a bit tired of the recurring investigations she was being asked to do. She felt it so unnecessary since the "robots" really were not robots but humans with unique abilities. "Well everything looks in order. I will begin investigation probably tomorrow."

"Please begin sooner since he will be okay to leave the hospital by tomorrow and he might be harder to track."

"I will try to accommodate but I need to finish my paperwork here first."

"Thanks, Marie."

The visual link and conversation ended.

Marie took a deep sigh as she walked toward her desk and lay the paperwork aside. Once seated she resumed her typing once again.

The sun shone through the window creating shadows on the floor and walls. Clicking of the keys and moans of frustration were echoing as the next two hours passed. Once the paperwork was completed Marie stored it on her personnel cloud drive.

"Now to get to the hospital ASAP."

Marie placed the paperwork inside the circle making a copy and digitizing it and then transferred the paperwork to her cell phone. The paperwork itself was placed inside a folder which she labeled Jim Boggs and placed alphabetically in the file cabinet in the corner.

Loaded with the data Marie grabbed her jacket, purse leaving the office. The door auto-locked as she left making a loud click. Walking down the hall to the elevator she remembered how robots came to be.

Early in 2003 after 911, the government began to realize that climate change was real. However, the economic problems of dealing with the issue made it more complicated. Using history as a guide, social economists saw that man could be heading into extinction through his own actions. In history it seemed like every time man made "progress" the environment was compromised. Many times the progress was actually the greed or power of a few dragging the populations into distress. Bad choices or policies made by those who were obsessed by greed and power created wars. To make weapons of war, forests were decimated to produce bows and arrows. It was the lack of forests to fuel the armies that drove some explorers to find the New World. Man has done more to nature to fulfill his desire for War, fueled by greed and power, than any other creature on earth. We are more of a danger to ourselves than any other species on earth could ever be to us.

Marie reached the elevator and pushed the down button. She found that to be symbolic of man. Always pushing buttons which just bring us down.

The elevator door opened. Inside the elevator was a projection on one wall resembling a television which recited ads and news in broadcast. As Marie entered, the ads and news began to flow. "I wish I could just shut them off." She thought as she closed her eyes to gather her thoughts.

It was a collaboration between social economics, science, and medicine that began the war on war. They knew that if we did not tame man's need for power and greed that we would drive ourselves and our world or maybe even our universe to extinction. But in order for it to work, all governments must work toward the goal as well. So how do they create man to survive and thrive without greed and power as their nature seems to be?

As they worked in silent, wars increased. Stock markets fell in 2007-2009, there were resets in 2014, 2015, 2016, and 2018. The big crash was in 2020. Economic instability caused by greed and power of a few. Climate change was finally viewed as real in 2020 when the weather systems became more erratic. Warming of the oceans, possibility of extinction of species was more acute, the general populations were being reduced due to wars, famine, disease, and pollution of the planet. Man, in his normal wisdom, went to war to try to reduce famine, disease and pollution, since he could not see that it was his own actions are what is causing the lack of food, energy, health, and destruction. It was always someone else's fault—not our own.

The elevator door opened and Marie stepped into the lobby of the office building. The huge glass octagon wall with revolving doors lay ahead. She moved quickly through the door toward the harbor and then toward the hospital.

Marie's thoughts continued to reemerge.

In 2020, after the crash, an opportunity peeked through the chaos. A secret meeting was held by the world's governments to try to stabilize our world. The social economics, science and medical representatives finally proposed a tentative solution. The governments only agreed to co-operate, only because of greed and power. They were told that the serum would give them more control over their populations. Thus they could retain their power and feed their greed and would no longer need wars. With no wars needed, our planet would we saved. Our populations would or could balance. With no wars needed the use of chemical warfare which poisoned our earth was not needed. Disease would be better controlled. Balance would be created. The earth's human and nature's population would be saved. And THEY would prosper.

Marie could see the hospital just ahead. She was tired of the lies told, that although it may be helping our existence, it was morally wrong.

She sighed as she stopped for a moment pondering how the investigation would go. "I will have to lie again."

As she began walking once again, the memories flowed.

The governments agreed to work with them but they wanted to make sure they were not being given false information. Thus, the Federal Bureau of Health was created in each country. They would gather information to make sure the serums worked and they could keep their greed and power.

Only a select few knew the truth and Marie was one of them. The doctors were not told because they could reveal it to the governments. Only the investigators knew the truth besides the social economic, medical, scientific community few who created the serum. If they tried to tell the secret without approval from within the group leaders, their brains would explode. Because each of them has an implant which is controlled by their own brains. The implant gets updates from the leaders when they are given the authority to speak or write the truth. So until an update is given, they must lie or die.

Knowing her life is on the line, Marie enters the hospital entrance and makes her way to the admission desk.

Chapter Four: The Meeting

"Hello, my name is Marie Gloss. I'm here to see Jim Boggs."

"Hello. Let me check what room he is in." The greeter entered Jim Boggs into the computer on her desk. "Oh, yes. Room 2020. Are you here to take him home?"

Marie was delighted to hear of this opportunity. "Why, yes. Do I need me to sign some paperwork?"

"Yes, sign here." The greeter passed an electric card for her to sign. After signing, the greeter gave her a key to his room. "Where shall I send the receipt of exit?"

"Just send it here." Marie gave her a business card with her contact information. "You may send it electrically."

Smiling at her good fortune, Marie gazed at the key. "This could be the key to my future." She thought as she entered the elevator to the 20th floor.

Once the elevator reached the 20th floor, she exited, looked for signage toward the room 2020. Turning right, she walked slowly down the hallway. The rooms all were enclosed but had large windows to view the patients from the hall. She suspected it made it easier for the staff to check up on them but it gave no privacy to the patients except for the curtains which could be closed.

Reaching the room, Marie saw Jim for the first time lying in his bed. He was rather handsome. "I wonder what his ability is." She thought.

Jim was bored. He was not used to staying in bed for long times and this was making him uncomfortable. "They told me I could leave today but never told me when." Murmured Jim. Then he heard a knock on the door. Looking up, he saw the most beautiful girl with blond medium length locks that curved on her face just enough to bring attention to her blueish green eyes peeking through the opened door.

"Hello, Jim. My name is Marie Gloss. I'm here to take you home."

"Take me home?" Jim was pleased. Just how lucky could he get? "Wonderful! I'm so tired of being here!" Jim sat up in his bed overjoyed to be leaving. Marie went to the small closet across the room, gathered his clothes and shoes and handed them to him.

"Get dressed. I will wait for you in the hall." Marie smiled, turned and left the room shutting the door behind her.

"Wow, not only do I get to go home but I can also spend some time with little beauty." He grinned from ear to ear.

Waiting in the hall, Marie was looking forward to the time she was to spend with Jim. She hoped she could obtain all the needed information. But as she looked at the key. "Could this key be it? The game changer? 2020?"

As Marie waited she soon was approached by a nurse with a wheel chair. "Are you Marie?" she asked.

"Yes."

"Good I'm glad I caught up with you. I need to wheel Jim Boggs out and I have this for you." The nurse handed her a clear plastic bag filled with instructions, medication, and prescriptions. "He should not go back to work for at least a week. He should make a follow-up appointment with Dr. Morris for a checkup and to get the final okay to return to work. His employer will need a signed release from him to return as well."

Just then the door opened and Jim emerged smiling but a bit off balance. "Whoa, Jim, please sit in the wheel chair so I can take you to the exit. "The nurse moved the chair near him and helped him into the chair.

Marie walked next to Jim as the nurse wheeled Jim into the elevator. "So, Marie. That is your name?" Jim asked. Marie nodded. "How are you getting me home? My car, I was told, was in an accident so I will assume it was towed somewhere. I do not know in what condition."

"I will call us a cab and take you home. Also I plan to stay with you for the first week to make sure you are okay. Thus I need to stop at my apartment and gather some clothes." Marie was liking how conveniently the situation lent itself to her needs.

"Staying with me? How did I get so lucky?" Jim asked. "Who do you work for?"

Thinking quickly she responded, "I work for a company who helps those injured and need help after they leave the hospital. It is covered in your insurance."

Jim looked perplexed since he did not realize that coverage was included. But he was happy it was. They entered the elevator and had to listen to the ads as they rode down toward the first floor. Marie lifted he phone and called a cab as they descended. Once they reached the lobby they were guided to the waiting room where the cab driver would be meeting them. The waiting room was busy with conversations but Marie and Jim were quietly waiting. The nurse had left them and was outside looking for the cab. Jim and Marie smiled at one another but both felt a bit awkward since they knew very little about one another.

Soon the nurse came inside. "Your cab awaits!" she announced as she grabbed the wheel chair and moved Jim through the door toward the cab. The driver helped the nurse lead Jim from the chair into the cab. "You take care!" she waved as she took the wheel chair back into the hospital.

Marie entered the cab from the other door and sat next to Jim. As the driver entered the cab and closed the door, Marie addressed him, "We need to stop at my place first. 1010 West Baltimore Street. I will just be a few minutes to gather my things and then we will go to Jim's home."

The driver nodded and set his meter. He also entered the address into his GPS. Then he turned on the engine by using his fingerprint. "I am still wondering how I got into a car accident. I thought our vehicles had auto breaks to prevent that." Jim said to try to get a conversation going.

"Just because you have auto breaks does not mean they can't fail." Marie smiled as she gave Jim quick glance. "Remember when they tried to have auto drivers? Machines can make mistakes and break. Humans can make choices but machines have to be programmed for every situation. The complexity of the machines became so expensive to create that no one could afford to buy them. Also trust in them waned when situations of frequent errors kept occurring."

"True. But I think they gave up too easily in trying. It would be nice to not have to drive ourselves." Jim replied.

"Don't you think that is a bit lazy? Man was not built to be lazy. For example, walking, eating, being active is what kept us healthy. It's also boring to let machines do everything for us."

"Yes, Marie, we are living creatures and thus we need to be active to keep us healthy. I just thought it would have nice to experience self-driving cars."

"Yes, and, was it not, the self-driving brakes that put you into the hospital?"

The cab driver pulled over to the curb. "1010 West Baltimore Street." He said as he turned around.

"Thanks. Please wait for me to return." Marie opened the door and rushed into the building.

"Pretty girl." The cab driver said looking at Jim. "How long have you two been together?"

Feeling a bit surprised, Jim said, "Not long. But you are right. She is a pretty girl."

"Would you like some music?" the driver asked.

"Yes. I would."

"Alexa, play, ABOUT TOWN"

The two men began to hum and then sing along with the music as they were waiting for Marie.

Marie quickly packed some clothes for her week's investigation. She called her office and asked Alexa to answer the phone by playing a recording that she was on assignment for a week but to leave a message. Then she packed her tooth brush, comb etc. in her small tote and left with the auto lock activated on her apartment.

Jim and the driver saw Marie pulling her luggage behind her as she exited the apartment building toward the cab. The driver left the cab and placed the luggage in the trunk as Marie entered the cab next to Jim. The music was still playing and Marie smiled as Jim continued to sing along.

The driver locked the trunk and entered the driver's side. "Now where to?"

Marie glanced at Jim. "2020 Belmont Plaza" Jim replied as he smiled and resumed singing.

"That is odd your hospital room number was the same number. 2020." Marie said as she wondered what was so important about that number.

"I guess you're right. You know your address was 1010. That is half of mine!"

They both laughed since the numbers probably do not mean anything.

Chapter Five: 2020

Once they reached Jim's abode, Marie gave the driver the fee via her credit card. "Wait a minute shouldn't I pay for that!" Jim expressed with a bit of alarm.

"Jim that is covered in your insurance." Marie said as the cab driver exited the cab to help Marie retrieve her luggage. Relieved that he was not breaking his masculine code, Jim open his door and proceeded to leave the cab. He was a bit wobbly so the driver happily helped him to his apartment as Marie followed with her luggage in tow.

They entered an elevator and went to the top floor. Marie was a bit surprised that Jim lived in the penthouse. After reaching the penthouse floor, they entered a small hallway which led to Jim's apartment. It seems his was the only penthouse apartment on the floor.

Jim reached for the entrance key where he placed his hand and eye on scanner. The door opened and they entered a large entranceway with a high ceiling which had rooms that branched forward, and left and right. "The bedrooms are to the left. You may use the one on the right. Mine is at the end of the hall." Jim pointed to Marie and the hallway as he spoke. "Please just take me to the living room. I want to sit down before I fall." The driver did as Jim requested as Marie moved her bags to her room.

Her room was very comfy. It had a small electric fireplace in the far corner of the room and the bed was against the right wall. There was a fantastic view of the bay from a large window, much like her office, which she enjoyed. Marie found the closet and began to unpack. She knew the next step was to get a conversation going about his childhood so she could begin to fill her report.

Once finished, Marie left her room to finding Jim in the living room looking through his mail which was delivered by enhancer daily and had piled up on his floor. It may have been only 3 days since his accident but he still had about 20 pieces of mail to sort through.

"Mostly junk mail." He said as Marie approached. "I will cinder it in a minute to recycle. So how do you like your room?"

"Very nice thank you. I love the view."

"Yes, it was the view that sold me on this place."

"How long have you lived here?"

"About 10 years. I moved here after my mom died."

"I'm sorry. I was not aware of your loss."

"One question. How did the insurance company know I needed someone to help me at home? I would have thought they would have asked."

"I guess they noticed you had no visitors and no one else on your policy. So is your dad alive? Siblings? Other relatives?"

"No. I never knew my dad. My mom had artificial insemination so I have no idea who he is or if he is alive. Mom never mentioned relatives either which I thought was odd. But she did spend a lot of time with me as a child. Her work allowed me to stay at a daycare center in the building where she worked."

"Nice. Not many places did that. Who did she work for?"

"Mom was a Doctor at the Federal Bureau of Health. Dr. Ruth Boggs. I am not sure what she did there."

"What was her birthday?"

"October 10, 2020. She never talked about her job or family. She said she had me when she was 25. I guess she did not find the right man to marry so she planned to have me on her own."

Marie was wondering if his mom was THE Dr. Ruth Boggs who was the first robot. It made sense she never married since she probably was forbidden to do so. As a test case, they might not want her to have split loyalties. Jim might be the second generation of robot or perhaps his mom kept his dad quiet due to the rules of no marriage she might have had.

"Have you ever had a geniality testing? That might help you find some relatives."

"No. Never thought about it. Why are you so interested in my genes?" He said with a smile.

A bit flushed, Marie answered, "I just thought you might be interested. I know I would. It would be nice to know who your dad was."

Jim nodded, "Yes that might be nice to know."

"So what do you do for a living?"

"Wow, the questions. "Jim was feeling a bit interrogated. "Currently I am working for Allied Chemical. But I have a variety of skills." He gave Marie a wink. Then he proceeded, "I worked as a mechanic from age 16-20. Then I went to college to please my mom. She wanted me to study medicine like her but I liked chemistry. While in school I worked part time as a landscaper, cook, and then began to invest in the stock market. Once I graduated I already had enough in investments to do as I pleased so I began to work as a chemist. It is more of a hobby than a job." He then looked at Marie, "Now tell me about you?"

Marie really was not prepared for an answer. She had to fudge some of the truth to avoid destruction. "Well, I know my parents. I have a sibling, a brother Daniel. Who works as, oddly enough, as a mechanic." Jim smiled to learn that tidbit. "I also went to college but I studied Law, Social Economics, and I, too, worked while in school. I worked in a diner as a waitress, then I was in sales, after which I did office work. My current job is helping people."

"So we both have had a variety of occupations." Jim smiled. "How about lunch?"

Marie returned the smile," Shall I cook for you?"

"No, I think today we will order delivery. Like Chinese?"

Chapter Six: New Plans

After Marie had gone to bed, Jim began to search the internet for robots. He was becoming more curious about what Dr. Morris told him. Marie had brought up some interesting points that he might want to take further. Marie never mentioned it but his mom's birthday is the numbers that reflect both his and hers addresses. Does that mean something? Perhaps Marie knows more than she admits.

Sadly the internet had only definitions relating to robots as machines. "I'm no machine." He thought. "But perhaps I am different—like my mom. She always seemed to know things before they happened. A sharp intuition. I have it somewhat but mostly regarding chemistry. But what yet do I have to learn?"

Jim closed his laptop. As he passed Marie's room he wondered if Marie was a robot like him. She said 2020 was repeating and I pointed out her address was half of mine. "Could just be nothing." He thought as he entered his bedroom to get some needed sleep.

Marie was awake by 7 am and began to complete her report on her phone. She still has not found what his "real" talents were. He said he had a variety of interests and knew mechanics, gardening, cooking, and finance but chemistry was his career. "I wonder what he is working on." Marie thought as she was filling in the report.

As she began to get dressed she heard Jim stirring in the hallway. "Are you awake?" Jim asked. "I plan to start breakfast. Want anything in particular?"

"Thanks Jim. I think I would like eggs with toast. Are you sure you don't want me to cook?"

"No, Marie, I am feeling better and how would you like your eggs?"

"Sunny side up."

Jim walked toward the kitchen wondering what kind of grilling Marie had for him today. She was rather questioning the day before. He began to open the refrigerator, pausing as he looked for the eggs. Grabbing the eggs he shut the door and reached for his skillet hanging over the center room counter where the sink also was placed. The stove was next to the refrigerator but it had counter top on both sides to maneuver as one cooked. Jim began to heat the stove and prepare the eggs.

After dressing and combing her hair, Marie left her room making her way to the kitchen. Today she might have to mention robots. She received her clearance to discuss them with him and that she knew he was one. Not knowing how that would be handled yet, she entered the kitchen.

"Good morning Jim! So you are feeling better today?"

"Yes. I am." Jim smiled as he gazed at Marie. "I decided to have eggs sunny side up as well. I hope you like whole wheat bread. I have it in toaster."

"Yes, whole wheat is fine. Anything I can help with?"

"No, I'm doing just fine."

The kitchen was a part of a large area which was sectioned off by how you would use it. Next to the Kitchen to the left was the dining area with a wall of glass with a door leading to the patio. On the right was the living room with a fireplace, TV, enhancer, sofa, some side chairs and coffee table, lamps the normal comforts. There was a bathroom off of the living room but tucked into a small hallway. Each bedroom had its own bathroom as well. The entrance way to the apartment led into this large living room area with the kitchen off to its left.

"We will eat in the dining room. You want to gather the utensils and place them on the table? Also the coffee pot is ready and don't forget the cups. The eggs are about ready." Marie got up and moved to the drawer Jim was pointing. She gathered the forks and knives placing them on the table. As she completed the task, Jim followed with plates for each of them filled with breakfast.

Sitting down Marie began to relish the smell of the eggs and toast. "This smells really good"

Jim also sat down smiling and began to eat. "So what do we have planned for today?"

"Well, the first thing, after cleaning up breakfast, is I want to check your surgery stitches to make sure they are healing. So I will probably be changing your dressings. Do you have your medications and have you been taking them?"

"Oh, yes, I opened the bag with the instructions in it. But I have not needed to take any pain killers yet today. I am hoping that is good news."

"Well, we will see once I remove your dressing. You did a great job with the eggs! Yum!"

Jim smiled once again as he continued to finish his meal. They glanced at one another as they quietly ate.

"Well I am finished." Jim placed his knife and fork on his plate and began to drink the coffee he poured from the pot on the table. "Want a refill" he asked Marie. She nodded as he poured her another cup.

"Looks like a beautiful day!"

"It sure is, Marie" but he was looking at her.

"Do you have to let your relatives know you are here?"

"No, Jim they live in another state."

"So you're not from Baltimore?"

"No, I grew up in West Virginia near the forests."

"Must be nice. I have lived in the city most of my life."

"You did mention your mom kept you in daycare at her job site. I take it they did not have an outdoors for you?"

"They had a playground but not the trees or forests you had. It's almost like I was caged. I had little freedom. Which is why I began to work at 16 doing mechanics. I needed to feel free"

"But you would still be inside—not in nature."

"True. But I could control where I went and what I did. Unlike the earlier years."

"Perhaps we need to take a trip to the forest. It might make you heal even more?"

"Great Idea! Can we go today?"

"Sure. After I tend to your wound. We can do a picnic!"

"No. How about a camping trip!"

"I'm not sure that is what the doctor ordered."

"I don't care. I want a camping trip!"

So they began to make their plans as Marie changed his dressing and checked his wound.

Chapter Seven: The Camping Trip Begins

After an evening of planning, Jim and Marie made plans to travel to Marie's family cabin in the hills of West Virginia. There, Marie thought, she could reveal some things she was holding back but now had permission to divulge to Jim. It might be a delicate thing to handle, so being away from other people might be a better place to educate Jim. Besides, she really missed the mountains and forest.

Fortunately, Jim found out his car was totaled. This meant that Marie could use her car for the trip. That would give her some control she might need later. Marie had left Jim to retrieve her car the next morning and gather some camping supplies. Jim was very excited and busy packing for the adventure. He had no clue what was in store for him but thought it would be fun and better than looking at the inside of his apartment until he was released to go back to work.

Later that day, around 10 am, Marie returned parking her car in front of the building. She locked her vehicle and rushed to Jim's suite where he was waiting anxiously.

"Jim, are you ready to go?" Marie yelled as she knocked on the door.

"You bet I am!" Jim said as he opened the door with a small rolling suitcase trailing behind him. "I packed what I thought I might need. I hope this is not too much." He turn around locking the door with the palm of his hand.

"No. Your fine." Marie smiled as she led him toward the elevator. As they rode toward the lobby both Marie and Jim were grinning from ear to ear.

"I feel like a kid again" Jim chuckled as they exited into the lobby and walked to the car. "Nice car! I ever expected you to have a small station wagon. I thought you were more of a sedan person."

Marie laughed and open the rear hatch. Jim lifted his case into the wagon and closed it. "Jim the front door should be open." Marie pointed toward the front passenger side. Jim nodded and rushed into the seat buckling himself in.

As Marie entered the driver's side she noticed another car across the street. The driver seemed to be watching as they as drove off. She kept looking in the rear view mirror to see if they were being followed. But it looked like the car stayed parked.

After a couple hours they were within a few miles of their destination. Marie wanted to get fuel and discreetly check for GPS trackers on her vehicle. Her intuition was firing ever since seeing the driver across the street from Jim's apartment house.

"Jim, I need gas and you might need a restroom stop as well. I know I do!" Marie said as she pulled into a small fuel station. Her vehicle ran on both gas & electric and she chose to load up on both. Jim left the car as Marie was attaching the electric and pulling the gas toggle. Once he was inside the building Marie scanned the outside of the car with her watch which had an app to check for devices on her car. It was given to her when she first became an agent of the FBH. Her superiors worried that she would be tracked and that might cause problems.

Sure enough she found 3 of them. She attached each magnetized GPS to other vehicles in the parking lot as a diversion and then quickly finished fueling. Just as she replaced the fuel ejectors Jim returned.

"Jim, I will make a quick run to the restroom." Marie said as she rushed toward the building. Jim sat quietly and waited for her return. It was less than 5 minutes before she was back. They left the station and began to continue on. To be safe, Marie chose to take several roads which did not lead to her cabin. It may add time on the trip but it was better to be safe.

After almost another hour, Marie drove up a large steep narrow mountain road. "Wow, this place is really out there!" Jim remarked as the trees hovered over the road hiding the light and sky.

Then Marie began to slow down and drove off to the side of the road in front of a large bush. "We're here." She announced as she exited the car. She then approached the bush and pulled it to reveal that the bush was attached to a gate. After opening the gate she returned to the car and drove it onto the dirt road which was on the other side.

Jim was stunned. "You're really are paranoid."

"Can't be too safe. We never wanted people to find the cabin because we knew they might rob us or harm us. There is no phone there. No electric. So we could be vulnerable." Marie got out of the car and replaced the bush gate to hide the entrance.

Jim was feeling a bit vulnerable. "Just who is she?" He thought. "What did I get myself into?"

Marie got into the car and began to drive for another mile. Then ahead on the right side of the road was a log cabin with a small porch in front. There looked like a small barn off to the side. Slowly they drove to the left side of the cabin and parked.

"Jim, relax. This is a hunting cabin. We needed it to be away from people so we would not accidently shoot someone. So having the entrance hidden is more for other people's safety. If they don't know we're here they won't accidently get shot."

Jim was not totally buying her explanation but it made him feel a little better because it did make some sense.

"Okay, Jim let's get the stuff out of the back and get things set up inside the cabin." Jim opened the door and made his way to the rear while Marie was leaving from her side and meeting him. She opened the hatch and they unloaded their bags and provisions setting them on the porch.

Marie made her way toward the door, pulled the keys from her pocket and unlocked the cabin door. As she walked in her steps could be heard as she walked across the wooden floor. "Well, it ain't much but it is better than sleeping on the ground." She paused for a moment. "And safer since bears have been known to be around here."

As Jim walked in carrying some of the bags and provisions he was a bit disappointed. It was not the vision he expected. The log cabin was just that. Logs were seen around the walls. A fireplace was on the back wall in the center of the room. It was a bit dusty and musty. There was a table on the left with four chairs and beyond a window over the rustic sink. There was a pump faucet on the right side of the sink which would be used to retrieve water from the well. There were 3 doors. One was off the kitchen area, and the other two were on the right. He did notice a wood stove which might be used for cooking as well as heat located closer to the far right doors. The kitchen area did have a propane barbeque grill on wheels.

Marie noticed his disappointment. "Jim, remember, this is a hunting cabin. Not a vacation resort. The door off the kitchen leads to the outhouse. "Marie opened the door to show a small hallway with a door at the end. She motioned him to follow. "Toilet will flush but you must remember to refill the top with a bucket of water from the kitchen when you finish. Toilet paper is here." She opened a closet where they were stored along with other items like broom, towels, medicine, and household supplies. "If we need to shower of wash we either gather water from the sink or we could visit the little pond in the back"

Feeling a bit over whelmed, Jim continued to follow her toward the other two doors. "Each one is a small bedroom. I will need to make the beds since they are just covered to keep away any dust when we are not here. But after a bit of straightening up you can choose which one you want."

They moved back into the main room. "This is where we relax. Don't mind the stuffed animals on the wall." She said as she pointed to the front inside wall where they entered. "That is dad's stuff. We can either use the fireplace or the woodstove if we need heat. I suggest we use the fireplace tonight."

"That sounds fine to me." Jim said as he smiled for the first time since entering the cabin. He turned and began to bring the rest of their things from the porch. "I don't see a refrigerator."

"No. None here. Which is why I have our perishables in the freezer box with the dry ice. That will get us through maybe 2 days at the most. So we need to smoke any meat we hunt to preserve it. I did bring propane for the grill and there may be more in the barn."

"Makes you wonder how pioneers did it. No refrigeration, electric, no gas, just wood and grit." Jim then opened a beer from the cooler. "Well, let's do this"

They spent the next two hours dusting, making beds, and starting the fireplace. Marie turned on the grill and began to make steaks. She had brought some vegetables and began to stir fried them. She had also bought some smoked meats that would keep once the dry ice was melted, canned foods, and snacks.

Jim was starting to blend in. He wanted this challenge. Now was his opportunity to see if he could live beyond the niceties of his youth and the wealth he later created. He always wanted to see how most of the world lived.

Jim chose the bedroom nearest the fireplace as his room. He moved his luggage inside and peeked out the window where he could see the front part of the barn. As he gazed at the trees he thought he saw something moving behind the brush. He kept his eye on the spot trying to see what was there.

"Jim, the steaks are ready!" Jim turned from the window and began to relish the dinner Marie had prepared.

Chapter Eight: Revelations

"Jim, chose a seat." Marie was busy placing the food in the middle of the candle lit table.

He chose the seat where he could view the front window and door. What was moving in the brush outside still bothered him but he was not going to alert Marie---at least not yet.

"Mmmm.... looks so good."

"I do hope you enjoy it." Marie decided that the conversation needed to be light at first. She planned to give some revelations to Jim and was not sure, yet, how he would accept them.

"Do you remember Julius Caesar?" Marie asked. Jim looked up a bit surprised by the question and topic.

"Yes, he was ruler of the Roman Republic and later assassinated by his senate elites." He responded wondering where this conversation was heading.

"Yes, he was assassinated by them but because they did not like his social and government reforms or his Julian calendar. He gave citizenship to far reaching regions of the Roman Empire, along with reform and support for veterans. Those actions angered the rich elite and they feared his "dictatorship to perpetuity". They felt they lost power."

"Okay. So where is this going?" Jim was puzzled by the entire point of the conversation and place his fork on his plate awaiting an answer.

"Well so much for light conversation" thought Marie. "I guess I screwed that up. Perhaps I just need to move on"

"Later there was Nero, Caligula, and several brutal rulers that came to power and later helped to destroy the Roman government because of their power and greed. The reforms were gone for the most part as men with power became addicted to that power."

Jim just sat there staring at Marie. Then he picked up his fork and took a bite of his steak. "Good steak, done just right."

"Thank you. I am glad you like it." Marie stopped talking for now and they just continued to eat their meal. The silence was deafening.

Jim arose after finishing his meal and began to move toward the sofa in front of the fire. "Just what was that conversation about, Marie?" Now feeling curious why she would talk about Rome dictators. Did she see him as one?

Marie lifted herself from her chair and moved the dishes into the sink. She planned to do them later since now seems to be right time for that conversation.

"Jim, I have something I must tell you. It will be hard to hear and I have to be careful how I tell you so I will not die."

"Die? You think I will kill you?" Jim gasped in horror. He never thought of hurting her and was horrified by her suggesting it.

"No, No, not you. I am not who you think I am. I have been given permission to give you more information but because of the implant in my skull, if I tell too much or don't lie it will kill me to protect secrets."

Shocked and amused by what seems like fiction Jim laughed and raised his arms. "You're not who I thought you were for sure. You're insane! You really want me to believe anything you tell me because you have an implant! "He paused when he saw tears in Marie's eyes. They were tears of sadness and fear. His voice whispered and calmed as he lowered his arms "You're not kidding are you? My God, who do you work for? Please, don't tell me, if they will kill you. I really would not like cleaning up that mess." He smiled as touched her cheek and admired her greenish blue eyes.

Marie smiled and chuckled a bit, "You just can't be serious can you?" Jim gave her a long hug. "Okay. Jim. Let's sit down on the couch where it is warm and I will try not to explode."

"Don't sit too close to fire just in case it acts as an accelerant on your implant." Jim joked as they sat.

"Remember when climate change was occurring in early 2000's?"

"Yes, it wasn't until 2020 that it was finally acknowledged it was really happening."

"Correct. It was then that man realized that he was contributing to the havoc by having wars, famine, disease, pollution of the planet and nations came together to solve the problem."

Jim heard this before from Dr. Morris. Was she going to tell him he was a robot as well? "Marie, I know."

"You know what?"

"I signed a paper not to tell anyone also. But no one told me I had an implant in my brain."

"Because you don't have one. Yes, you, are what they call a robot." Jim smiled since he did not have to say it. "But their definition is not the real one."

Jim kept gazing into Marie's eyes as she explained how the robots got their name since the all-powerful and rich wanted to retain their power by manipulating man's genes so they may control them. She explained how she worked for the Federal Bureau of Health as an investigator who reported back to the rich and powerful, to insure them, that they indeed had control over their robots.

"But the thing is. The scientists actually changed your genes to have powers and to be able to keep your control and when there was enough born, they can gain control over the tyrants. But we must be careful not to become addicted to power just like them or the world will be even worse than before."

After hearing the tale Jim was a bit overwhelmed. "So I am a bit superior? Cool. What are my talents?"

"That is what I brought you here to find out."

"Are you one as well?"

"Yes."

"So how did they create us?"

"Remember flu shots?' Jim nodded. "Well they were also infused with a small serum beginning in 2020. That continued until recently when they came up with a lifetime dose. Actually, as far as the flu is concerned, they just increased our immune system to fight more illnesses like curing cancer and others."

"Yes, I wondered about that. How could people think that artificial things would be healthy for us? Healthy food, exercise, and balance were the best since it improved our immune system. How could anyone think that harmful radiation was better than letting our bodies fight by increasing our own immune strength?"

"I know, it was like the bloodletting which killed people. Logic says we need our blood, yet the modern medicine of the times did not see the obvious. It is the same now. People still don't see power and greed as addictive. They see it as success. The few who have it see no problem in destroying others and the world to feed their addiction."

"So now what?" Jim asked.

"Tomorrow we begin to find your talents."

They began to rise after their long discussion and began to retire to their rooms.

"Marie, by the way, I thought I saw movement in the brush near the barn earlier. I forgot to tell you."

"Not to worry. It was probably a bear." Marie smiled and entered her room.

Jim, not feeling at ease with that revelation, stopped for second after hearing that word BEAR. Then proceeded into his room to get some rest.

Chapter Nine: Nature

Jim had tossed and turned throughout the night. Every little noise sounded odd to him and made him nervous. Since living his life inside his mom's work location and later the city, he got used to hearing cars, machines, whistles, and other noises at night. The silent noises of the forest were unfamiliar. Hooting, bussing, tweets, howls, the wind brushing the trees were odd to him.

The cabin had some blinds in the windows which hid the contents but still allowed the sun to shine into the room as dawn approached. A bit of light spit through the side of the blind and landed right on Jim's eye as he lay in bed. Then a little fly buzzed above his face and landed on his nose. Jim felt its touch and suddenly awoke from his sleep and slapped himself. "Ouch! That hurt!" Jim yelled as he sat up in bed. "Not exactly a good night's rest. Flies. I hate flies." He then heard movement outside his door. "I hope that is Marie and not a bear." He groaned as he turned rubbing his eyes, yawning. "Just what time is it?" He reached for his wrist watch resting on the side table. "Five AM! I need more rest."

Suddenly there was knocking on the door. "Jim are you okay? I heard you yelling about being hurt."

"Yes, I'm fine. Just awakened by an annoying fly."

"Good. Glad you're okay. Ready for breakfast?"

Jim sighed, yawned, and stared at the door. "Okay. But isn't it a bit early to be up?"

"No. Not at all. We have a lot to do today. Eggs and toast?"

"Fine." He whispered.

"Jim, eggs and toast?"

"FINE!" he repeated louder as he fell backwards on the bed and moaned.

Marie quickly began fixing breakfast humming and then singing. After a few minutes Jim opened the door to his room peeking out. He saw Marie busy and happily singing as she worked. "She is a wonder." He thought as he then exited his room and made his way to the table. "Coffee?" he asked groggily.

Marie smiled and poured him a cup as he sat down. Jim reached for the cream on the table and poured a bit into his cup as he stirred. "So what is in store for us today?"

After placing their plates filled with food on table in front of each of their chairs, Marie, sat next to Jim. "Ever shot a gun?"

"Actually no. Being in the city, guns were prohibited. And since I never left the city…."

"So today we will hunt. We need to gather meat and smoke it for preservation since we do not have a refrigerator."

"What kind of meat are we hunting for?" Jim asked as he munched his food.

"Whatever nature offers us."

After breakfast Jim helped with washing the dishes and reluctantly replenished the toilet after using it.

Marie and Jim walked to a trunk located below the stuffed heads and opened it. Inside were a variety of weapons. Bows and arrows, antique guns which used old bullets, and the newer laser guns which needed no ammo since they run on self- generated power. "Wow! What a collection! So what will be use?"

"I think the laser since it allows us to not have to carry ammo with us. We will be walking into the woods and need to be as agile as possible. We also need to bring this game carrier." She lifted a large bag and rope. "Depending on what we kill and where, we might need to lug or drag it home. This bag has elevation technology to replace wheels. It will make it easier to return our prey."

Jim was impressed with her thought process. She then handed him a laser gun. The gun was about one foot in length and a little bulky but easy managed. It had a belt that could be hung over the shoulder in transport or worn around ones waist. Marie chose one similar to his and then shut and relocked the trunk.

"Before we go I need to give you a lesson on how to use it." Marie led him to the other side of the barn where a small shooting range was set up. She proceeded to show him how to unlock, aim, and shoot. Then how to relock. Jim was amazed at how silent the gun was. He was used to old movies where loud noises pierced the air as bullets flew. But these were silent due to the fact it was run by light. Light is silent. The only sound heard was from the target hit-not the weapon. It wasn't long before Jim was hitting the target and at ease with the laser.

"You're doing quite well Jim." Marie smiled as she was a bit surprised at the ease Jim took to target practice. "Now we need to gather our belongings and set forth!" She smiled as she waved Jim onward feeling a bit playful.

"Gather our belonging's and set forth!" Jim laughed. "What movie are you playing in?" He lifted his small back pack and slung it over his shoulders as Marie did and then followed her in que with his laser.

They began to walk down a small path which began across the road from the cabin. The thick, tall, trees hovered over them as they moved down the sloping path. As they paced, the brush began to thicken. Owls where heard in the branches above as well as birds chirping. But for the most part it was quiet. A silence Jim had never heard. It made him a bit uneasy but also relaxed at the same time. A weird feeling for sure.

"Marie, can we get lost?" Jim anxiously asked.

"We could….but I know where we are and where we are going." Jim was not amused with that answer. He was used to being in control and felt out of place.

Marie, who was leading the way, stopped and raised her hand over her head. She turned around and gave Jim a motion with her finger over her mouth to be silent. Jim stood there listening. He could see and hear some motion in the bushes just ahead. Marie crouched down signaling for Jim to follow her actions. As they crouched a gruff noise was heard. Then a yelp of some sort. Then out of the brush came a momma bear with a cub. "Don't move." Marie whispered. Jim was both fearful and in awe as the bears strolled across the pathway oblivious to them. Marie whispered, "We need to make sure they are gone before we proceed." As they sat crouched Jim placed his hand gently on hers and stared into the woods. Marie was a bit startled at first at him touching her but soon relaxed feeling a bit smitten with his gesture.

"Okay. We can continue now." Marie spoke as she arose.

"Out of curiosity, knowing we are hunting, why did we not hunt the bear?" Jim asked now standing next to her. "Was it because it was too dangerous?"

"No. It was a mom and cub mostly. We need to allow nature to breed and grow, otherwise, we doom ourselves as well."

Chapter Ten: Talents

Marie's words "We must let nature breed and grow or we too are doomed" echoed in Jim's mind as they continued down the path. "If that is true...why are we hunting? Why not just buy some food a store near us instead? Why kill if we don't need to?" Thought Jim.

The forest opened up and they were able to see a large lake at the bottom of the path. "Wow!" Jim exclaimed. "How beautiful!"

"Glad you like it." Marie smiled. "How about fishing instead?"

"Great. But how does that work? We have no poles?"

Marie reached inside her pack and showed Jim a ball of fishing line. "We just need our make our own pole and attach a line."

They reached the water where they found some dead branches that could be made into poles. Marie showed him how to bait the hooks, she brought as well in her backpack, with some worms she dug up nearby in the woods. Soon they were walking barefoot into the lake and tossing their lines. It wasn't long before Jim got a bite on his.

"Is this how I do it?" Jim asked as he gave the pole a sudden yank and the fish began to fight.

"Yes, you got it!" Marie laughed as she watched Jim smiling with joy as he pulled in his fish.

Just then Marie also got a bite and yanked on her pole and was laughing and yelling as she pulled in hers as well. They both caught about 3 fish each and called it a day.

As they made their trek back to the cabin Jim asked, "Marie, how come it was so easy to catch the fish?"

"Well, the lake is rarely fished anymore. It is hidden and on our private property. Therefore the fish aren't wise to our methods. Nature, like us, learns what is dangerous through experience. If they never see the danger, they can't avoid it."

"Why do we hunt when we can find food at the store? We can get more canned food and don't have to hunt." Jim wanted to understand or find an answer to his thoughts.

"You're right. The only drawback to our canned food is the same one we had historically. Safety. Still today, much of our food is grown, harvested, and raised by man who, unfortunately, still has not learned that overkill to make money, instead of just feeding people is a problem. Then, in order, to gain time to sell what they over killed or harvested, they had to create processes which change the true value of the food into more of non-food or create cans contaminated with mercury."

"But aren't there some food preservations that are good? Like freezing?"

"Yes, but we have no refrigerator here. Smoked foods work because we don't add chemicals."

"Being a chemist, I see your issue. Perhaps I need to focus on something that is more like nature to preserve food as well."

"That would be nice. Is it possible?"

"Perhaps. Natural preservatives are Lemons, garlic, Himalayan Rock Salt, Fermented foods, cayenne, hot sauce, and mustard. I might be able to ....."

"Just do it without changing the natural structures." Marie interrupted.

"Right. I need to BE nature." Jim smiled realizing he now has purpose.

"Jim, if you can do that....it would or could save nature and man. Perhaps, that is one of your talents."

"By the way, what are your talents, Marie?"

"Watch." Marie said with a smile as she raised her arm and an owl came and perched itself on her arm. Jim was stunned. "I can talk to the nature. Thankfully I can control it so when I need to hunt or harvest so does not interfere."

"Does that mean ALL nature? Including humans?" Jim grinned at the thought.

"Unfortunately or fortunately, yes." Marie laughed, "Stop it, Jim. I can almost hear your thoughts"

They were still laughing as they reached the cabin. "I need to start a smoker fire to preserve the fish. Meantime, take two of these and clean them so we can fry them for dinner."

Jim gave her a puzzled look, "Clean them? How?"

"Don't try that with me, Jim, you know perfectly well how to gut and clean the fish. Slice it open, take out the insides, and wash it."

"Jim laughed. "Yes, I know. I just wanted to make sure you knew...I knew" Jim grabbed two of the fish and entered the cabin.

Chapter 11: Preservation

Marie planned to smoke the fish until it was dehydrated and became jerky. That way they would have a food source they could use minus a refrigerator. That process would take several hours. So she was busy making the fire and kept it going but tried to maintain the heat to dry the fish out after it was cooked. Meanwhile Jim cleaned & washed the other fish and began to pan fry it with seasoning inside the cabin.

"Marie! Fish is ready!" Jim yelled from the cabin.

Marie, satisfied that the fire was contained, arose from her bench near the fire. "Coming!" she shouted. Once inside the cabin they sat and began to eat their bounty. "Looks good, Jim"

Jim grinned and tasted his meal. "Yum. I really like this."

"Well you did a good job with the cooking." Marie was enjoying the meal as well. Thinking it was not the time to ask questions, this time she just ate her meal.

After they had finished, they cleared the table. "Jim, I thought we would sit outside near the fire this evening. That way I could also check on the fish as we view the stars. It is looking like a good clear night."

"Sounds good to me." Jim was appreciating the experience. Growing up he rarely got to see nature in the way this trip was. "Maybe you could tell me more about your "talents"." Jim thought.

Marie and Jim walked toward the fire. The large bench with a back could hold 2-3 people. They sat next to one another as Marie was feeding the fire as needed. The sun was slowly setting casting deep shadows from the trees. The birds chirping ebbed as the crickets began to sing. Slowly the fireflies glinted and flashed giving a sparkle to the woods.

"Jim, did you know your grandparents?"

"No. Mom said she was left on the steps of an orphanage with a note just giving her birthdate."

"I'm so sorry."

"No. I know nothing of relatives, since, neither did my Mom. Genetics don't give you that information. And with nothing but birthdate ..."

"Couldn't the authorities use the birth date to find her mom?"

"No. They think the birth was not made in a hospital due to some of the birth cord was still attached."

"So, was she later adopted?"

"Yes, sort of." Jim winced. "The orphanage was her parents until age 18. Then the FBH, who founded the orphanage, asked her to work for them. They became her family. And later myself as well." He sighed. "So I really have no interest in or way of determining my ancestry...at least by a person other than my Mom."

"But what about your dad? Can't your Mom track down him? I would think they had a record of that when the person gave their sperm."

"Yes, maybe, but I really don't NEED to know. The way man has used science to change our genes for the last 100 years, we are so far from being true humans anymore. We are more man made. As we go down that path who knows if anyone will have different genes anymore. That might be a problem if we lose our adaptability in the process."

"I agree. I wonder if the progress in genes is more about making us ONE than allowing us to be diverse." Marie was a bit surprised that Jim, a chemist, questioned this.

Jim noting Marie's surprised look remarked, "I know sounds odd coming from me. But I have been thinking about this for some time. I just have not expressed it until now. I worry that man will progress himself out of existence. Nature has always been in control and had been doing just fine. But since we have interfered we have lost so many species. We seem to forget that we depend on other species to exist."

"What if I could find out who your father was?"

"You think you could?"

"Maybe."

"I'm not sure I want to know. He obviously did not want to be a dad, only a donor."

Marie glanced at the fire and checked the fish. They were now dry enough and had become jerky. She arose and removed them to a basket with a cloth liner. "Jim, I am really tired. So I will take these in and head to bed. She then bent over and kissed Jim gently on the lips and walked into the cabin.

Jim sat stunned. "What just happened? Did Marie just kiss me?" He then smiled as he poured water on the fire to safely put it out. Looking up at the stars which glowed like glitter thrown about the universe. "I wonder what is in store tomorrow?"

Chapter 12: The Crack

As dusk arose the sun began to peep into their bedroom windows. Outside the bushes were stirring. Then a sudden loud crack echoed waking Jim and Marie who both arose with a start in their beds. Marie rushed to the window and slowly pulled the drape a pinch to try and determine what happened. As she did, Jim rushed into her room and then whispered, "What was that?"

"I'm not sure. I can't see anything."

Jim positioned himself behind Marie so he, too, could see out the window. But nothing obvious jumped out.

"Maybe it was a tree falling." Marie said as she turned toward Jim. It was then she realized she was in her nightgown and grabbed her blanket to cover herself.

Jim never noticed her grabbing the blanket since he was still watching the forest for clues. "Guess we could check it out later?" he asked.

"Yes, we could." Marie felt a bit uncomfortable. "Jim, could you leave and let me get dressed?"

Surprised by that statement Jim nodded and awkwardly left the room. He then returned to his room to get dressed as well.

After several minutes they were both clothed and made their way to the dining area. Marie began to make the coffee as Jim sat down. "Marie, could we check it out this morning?"

"Sure, but after breakfast. Egg sandwich?"

"Okay. I'm a bit disturbed by the loudness of that crack. Do trees always make that sound?"

"No not always. But my issue is what caused the tree to fall? An animal, person, or just old age?"

"Could we be... are we being watched?"

"It is possible. On the way here I found some trackers on our vehicle." Jim looked up a bit shocked. "But I placed them on other vehicles when we got gas. I also suspected a car was following us when we left your house. I did lose them ...or at least I thought I did."

"Why didn't you tell me?"

"I thought I could handle it."

"Well, now we both need to handle it." Silence followed as they just looked at one another.

"What do they want?" Jim continued as he ate his meal.

"I think they may be checking on me...or both of us. They may be other FBH people or part of another group of spies paid for by the governments to check up on the job the FBH is doing. They are really paranoid that their mission of control via robots is not secure."

"From what you told me, with good reason." Jim retorted.

"Yes, I guess so. It feels like a chess game."

"Just how good are you at chess, Marie? I'm not too bad." Jim grinned as he attempted to add some levity to their situation.

"Jim, you just can't be serious can you?" Marie laughed as she felt some calm over his humor.

They finished their meal, grabbed their back packs and lasers, and moved toward the woods from where the crack came.

The sky was darkening as clouds formed above. A storm was coming but neither of them seemed to notice. "Jim try to walk heel then toe to maintain your footing better but if we need to be quiet, then walk toe then heel and crouch but be careful for traps." Marie instructed as she entered into the bushes from where the crack came.

"Traps?" Jim asked. "Why would there be traps? Did you set them?"

"No. But if others want to harm us, they might."

As they proceeded along they noticed broken foliage ahead of them. Marie motioned for Jim to be quiet and walk stealthily. Crouching below the brush as they moved forward, the muffled sound of voices were heard. Soon they found themselves atop a cliff. When they peered down from where the sound was coming, two men were seen below. They each had rifles and seemed to be resting. Marie motioned Jim to be quiet and still. The men's voices were echoing along the cliffs and Marie was trying to hear their conversation.

"Are you sure we should be here? Doesn't this land belong to someone?" One man asked.

"All land belongs to someone. But no one is here so we should be okay to hunt." Another replied.

Marie smiled as she whispered to Jim, "They are hunters. They also do not know who owns the land. So we can assume no threat. I think I will just let them hunt. Let's go back."

"Did they make that crack?" Jim asked.

"I don't think so. But we can let them alone and look elsewhere. They are not an issue."

Marie and Jim then moved back toward the path from where they veered before they saw the broken foliage. Once back to the path they proceeded further along the path looking for fallen trees or anything that might have been the sound of the crack. After a few minutes they did see a tree which had fallen across the path and went over to inspect it.

"Marie, this tree could have been it." But them Jim noticed the tree was chopped down with something like an axe. "Marie, this was no dead tree. This was purposely cut. But why?"

As Marie inspected the tree she closed her eyes and seemed to go into a trance. "Marie, are you okay? Marie?"

Suddenly Marie opened her eyes. "Those men chopped it down. But that makes no sense."

"How do you know they chopped it?"

"I asked nature." Marie looked a bit frightened. "Jim, I might have been wrong. They might not be hunters of game—but people."

"What do you mean?"

"Sometimes there are men who release people into the woods to hunt them. I know it sounds cruel and criminal and you are right, it is. But unfortunately they do exist. But I never thought our property was used for this." Marie paused. "We need to get back and report it to the police."

Quickly they turned and began to make their way back to the cabin. When they arrived and entered the cabin it was ransacked. Her father's antique weapons were gone. The car was there but the tires had been slashed.

Jim and Marie had a look of panic on their faces. "Jim, we need to get out of here and back to the town. We're in danger."

Chapter 13: Evil Incarnate

Page | 91

Marie and Jim began to walk quickly down the dirt road, which they used when entering, looking cautiously as they went. The sky had darkened even more as the wind was getting stronger and a chill filled the air.

"Marie, how does that cut tree bring that theory into your mind?"

"When I was a child my dad would tell us about it around the campfire. He would say they would begin by cutting a tree across a path to mark the beginning of the hunt. Once the hunt was over, the tree was used to burn the corpse or corpses and feast on some of the flesh of the prey."

"How do you know that story is true? It could have been just a story."

"If you saw my dad's eyes as he spoke…it was the truth. He had fear in them."

"So what about the ransacked cabin? It couldn't have been the hunters… we just saw them in a different place."

"There might be more than one hunting pair or they might be the prey looking for weapons or other items for survival. My dad's cabin is rarely used anymore since he died. So guess that is why they chose this property. "

"If it was the prey, so why didn't they just take the car and leave?"

"They don't have the keys but they might have thought the car belonged to one of the hunter pairs and chose to disable it."

Looking up at the sky Marie pointed to the side of the road. "The rain is coming soon. It looks like a bad storm. Follow me."

Jim followed into the bush along the road and a few feet from the road was a small hidden cave like structure in the hill. They entered just as the rain began to pour.

"We can hide here until the storm passes." Marie said as she sat on a rock inside the small overhang. Jim sat next to her feeling a bit overwhelmed.

"I'm so sorry to get you into this situation, Jim. I had no idea about the hunters. I thought perhaps the FBH was the issue but they are not as dangerous as the hunters."

"How are they different? They both might be willing to kill us."

They sat quietly as the storm was raging. Jim was feeling afraid and sad. So he thought some more conversation might help. "Marie, I am sorry about your dad. Is you mom alive?"

"No. She died before dad."

"So you are an orphan like me?" He reached over gently took her hand.

As the storm began to pass they remained quiet and continued to watch for signs of hunters. Soon the wind died and the rain ceased but the sky was still gloomy and dark.

"I think we can continue on. We're about a half mile from the gate." Marie stood making one last glance before stepping slowly and quietly onto the dirt road. Jim followed and caught up with her. Together they made their way to the gate. As they got closer, Marie placed her index finger over her mouth as she entered the brush on the side of road and motioned Jim to follow. "We need to be very careful. They might be guarding the gate." She whispered. "If we see them there we will need to by-pass the gate and trek through the brush and over the hill to get to the highway. We want to avoid using our lasers, if at all possible. Killing people is them not us."

Sure enough there were two guards at the gate carrying guns. They were sitting in the brush trying to hide and catch their prey. Marie and Jim looked at one another, pulled their lasers from their belted cases and began to slowly and carefully move through the brush. Jim could feel his body changing. The fear was something he never experienced before. The fear grew as they kept moving forward. Then suddenly Marie stepped on a small branch which let out a loud snap. She stopped. The men at the gate heard the snap and got up to see what had caused the sound. Jim's fear had grown so powerful that he could barely breathe. He noticed his skin felt prickly and sweat was dripping down his forehead. Marie remained still and began to internally pray.

As the men stood, they kept looking where Jim and Marie were, awaiting some hint as to what was moving. Then one of the men cocked his gun and began to move closer toward the brush. It was at this point that Jim's fear suddenly changed. Much like the flick of a switch, instead of fear all he could feel was rage. A feeling of power and invincibility came flowing throughout his entire body. Jim released his laser. Lifting his arms and forming fists, he ran out from the brush knocking the gunman down and then with a wave of his hand he lifted the other man into the air and threw him 20 feet. Both men were knocked out and laying on the ground.

Marie stood stunned by what she saw. This calm, gentle man became a superior fighter. Jim, himself, was taken by surprise. Looking back at Marie he calmly spoke. "I guess I can fight." Marie smiled and laughed. "Yes, you can. I guess that is another talent you have!"

They both smiled as Jim retrieved his laser and they opened the gate running down the road toward town.

Chapter 14: Practice Makes Perfect

Running down the mountainous road was a bit harder than Jim expected. He thought downhill would be easier than uphill but they were both strenuous. Downhill you had to brace yourself for falling since the balance was off with the grading. Uphill was exhausting since you were pulling yourself relentlessly. This road that went downward had a lot of uphill as well due to some of the turns and their angles.

"Marie, why in God's name, did they build the roads in this weird way?" Jim stopped at the side of road leaning against the tree to get his breath. "I need a bit of a rest."

Maries stopped, turned and walked back to Jim. "In winter the road can be treacherous. Building it with some slope or occasional flatness would give vehicles some brace in snow and ice. The roads here do not get plowed or salted like in the city. They do some plowing but not as often and, instead of salt, which too much can endanger the wildlife, they use cinder from their fireplaces, if possible, which enrich the soil. It might not look good but it is healthier for the plant life."

"They have THAT much cinder here?"

"No, not as much as before. Some of the cinder was from coal in the past. Now they still occasionally use it but not as much since coal is not used as our major energy source anymore."

"Is coal used in place of cinder?"

"If finely ground it can be used instead of salt. But even if coal is more natural like other rocks, people in cities want to retain the whiteness of the snow with salt and want the salt to melt away.

The coal won't melt, darkens the snow and can clog up sewers etc. But here, it can work fine. The coal can work its way back into the dirt roads and melt in that way." Marie paused as she gazed at the sky. "Come on we need to reach town before the night comes. This cloudy weather could bring more rain."

Jim, still panting, nodded and began moving down the road once again with Marie.

"By the way Jim. Can you explain that wave of the hand move that tossed that gent 20 feet?"

"No. I can't."

"It looked like you did it without effort. Almost like you did not even touch him."

"Yes." Jim stopped for a moment and then caught up with Marie. "I really did not touch him. I...."Jim hesitated. "I just thought about moving him away."

Marie stopped with a stunned look on her face and then caught up with Jim. "Jim THAT is your talent."

They both stopped and looked at one another. "But how did I do it? I don't know if I can repeat it."

"We need to think about the trigger. How did you feel when you were doing it?"

"Invincible, angry, after, I'm ashamed to admit, a strong sense of fear."

"I think the fear awakened your talent. To repeat it you should not have to experience that fear again but just remember the combined feeling it created. If you can control that feeling at will, your power will truly be yours."

"Do we practice?"

"We can or rather you can---but in a safe environment to protect you and others. Can you remember it?"

"Yes, it was very profound. What was your awakening moment, Marie?"

"Mine was also a combination of fear and anger. Which is why I thought yours was the also the trigger. I was very young, about 7 or 8, it started with the campfire story dad told. That night around the fire, the story about the hunters haunted me. In the middle of the night I thought I heard them coming for me. My fear was immense. Then suddenly the fear went away, I also felt anger. Then I talked to nature. I asked them if the danger was real and what I should do. Nature told me all was well and I had nothing to fear."

"But it told you differently today?"

"Yes. Which is why I knew we were in danger."

"Well you were right."

"Jim, take a moment and try to recreate the feeling you had. Then try and move some brush or tree limbs. But try to move them gently. You need to control it. Not let it control you."

Jim stopped, closed his eyes and remembered the feeling from before. Then he opened his eyes and waved his hand very gently and slowly in the air as he thought about the tree branches which were about 20-30 feet away across the road. They watched as the limbs moved back and forth to mimic the movement of his hand. "How cool is that?" Jim said. Then he suddenly moved his hand without thinking and a tree limb broke falling with a loud crack and fell to the ground rolling onto the road. "Oops. " Jim winced. "I've got this," he said with a grin. He then used both hands in motion to lift the branch and move it into the brush a bit deeper into the woods and off the roadway.

"You're doing great! Good move." Marie grinned as she patted Jim on the shoulder.

"Now… how do I shut it off?"

"Think of happiness and breathe deeply. It should calm you and release."

Jim followed her advice and thought of happiness while breathing deeply. Then he tried moving his hands to see if it worked. "Well I did not move anything or destroy anything. So I guess I'm turned off."

"See. You do have talent."

Jim continued to practice turning it on and off as they continued on their trek to town, as Marie kept checking with nature to make sure the hunters were not following them.

Chapter 15: The Town Police

About an hour later they could see the town below them in the distance. It was situated along a river and surrounded by forest. The sky was still a bit hazy but occasionally a beam of sunlight pierced through and would highlight various spots on the land below. The road was no longer dirt but asphalt. The traffic was slowly increasing as they made their way to the outskirts of town. Marie glanced at her watch for the time. "The police station is not too much further ahead. It is 2 o'clock and they should still be in full force. They only have a couple of men who stay there after 5 o'clock."

Both Marie and Jim were exhausted after the long hike but very happy to see the police sign hanging in front of a building just ahead. The town was busy but not crowded. People were walking along the sidewalks, entered and exiting their cars, the shops, and some restaurants. Some were walking their dogs and others were carrying bags or engrossed in conversation while walking or sitting on an occasional bench. The electric street lights along the sidewalks were modeled after the old time gas lights in old English novels. Except for the pedestrian and automotive control lights, the town looked like it was fashioned after eighteenth century architecture.

When they reached the police station door, they had to walk up three steps to the door landing where they entered the station. There was a small waiting area with seats within the room. At the end of the room was where the police greeter was seated at his desk. They saw other rooms with eye view windows into the waiting room with doors that would close for some voice privacy.

Marie led the way and stopped in front of the greeter desk. "Hello. Can you help me?" She asked.

The policeman looked up and gazed at her with surprise. "Marie?"

"Why yes. How do you know me?"

"Just a moment." The policeman ran to the room marked Chief of Police and knocked on the door. "Sir. I think you want to come out and see this visitor."

The Chief of Police glanced out the window where he could view the waiting area. He then smiled, got up, open the door and walked out toward Marie. "Marie? Marie? Is that you?"

She stared at the Chief a moment then smiled, "Dan? What are you doing here?"

"I am the Police Chief. I work here."

"But what happened to your mechanic job?"

"I ended that and began to work for the department after dad died. I tried to get in touch with you but the FBH refused to help me. They said you were on a mission and could not be interrupted."

"That was over five years ago. I could not get in touch due to my job. Actually I am still doing that same job. But I am glad we met. Wow! Police chief. We have a lot to catch up on." Marie was a bit in shock. She had missed so much of her personnel life since the FBH demanded so much. She had been forbidden to contact relatives or have a life beyond the job. They were so paranoid of her.

"And you are?" Dan asked Jim.

"Jim, I am a friend of Marie's." Jim said as Dan and he shook hands.

"Can we talk in your office Dan? I need your help and can't talk out here." Marie whispered as she gazed about the station.

"Sure, my office," He said with pride as he led them in and motioned to some chairs inside for them to sit. "Have a seat. I have so much to tell you as well."

"Ladies first," Jim motioned for Marie to choose a chair and waited for her to sit before he sat down. He then focused on Dan, "Nice office you have here. Looks well run."

"Thank you. How long have you known my sister?"

"A few days actually."

"A few days?" Dan was a bit puzzled.

"Dan, Jim is a client. But we are becoming good friends as well." Marie interjected not wanting to put Jim on the spot. "I took him to the cabin on FBH business and then..." she whispered, "the hunters came. They ransacked the cabin, slashed the tires on my vehicle, and we have been running from them. You need to send some officers up there to clear them out and help me get my car tires replaced to we can continue our work."

"The FBH has no jurisdiction here. But it is our family property so I will send officers up there to clear it up. I personally will check out your car and see it gets back to working order. Meantime you can stay here in town until I can get your car ready. I may have to tow it to a local shop to replace the tires. Do you have clothing etcetera that you need from there?"

"Yes, we do. Dan? Can we go with you to tow the car and get our things?" Marie asked.

"Okay. But let's wait until I have the place cleared of the hunters." Dan then whispered, "You know the hunters are probably local folks. So I need to be careful how I handle it. I don't need a local war."

Marie nodded and glanced at Jim who was looking a bit uneasy. Dan then left the room and signaled some policemen to gather in another room where he then gave them instructions. The men left gathering their guns. Dan then returned to his office. "They will clear it. Once it is done, we can get your car and belongings. It might take a couple hours. Why don't you visit the restaurant down the street for a while? I need to finish paperwork here. Although we are used to seeing people with guns around town due to the hunting season, you might want to try and hide them when you're out walking. " Jim and Marie stood, shook Dan's hand and left the station heading for the restaurant.

Jim and Marie placed their weapons inside their jackets. "Marie. How trustworthy is your brother? I only ask because he does not seem as upset about the hunters. Could he be aware of them? Could he be one?"

"Jim. I thought the same thing. I often wondered if my dad was one of them. I don't want to dwell on it. If we can get our car and belongings I don't plan to go back there any time soon. It is a nice place but if it is being used in that way—well I need to find another space."

Chapter 16: The Cabin

Three officers arrived at the gates to the Gloss property in the police car. They did not run their sirens to alert the intruders. One cop got out of the passenger side of the car, peeked into the gate bush, and then slowly opened the gate. No one was seen so far. They moved their vehicle slowly through the gate and parked waiting for the policeman to close the gate behind them. As the cop entered the car the others were very alert to any sounds or sights which surrounded them.

"Bill," the driver said as he put the car in gear, "did you see any signs of intrusion?"

The copper sitting next to him gave him weird look. "Dave, I would tell you if I saw anything. So no, I did not see anything."

Joe in the back seat gave both of them a stare. "Are you guys going to start this again? Can't the two of you stop bantering one another?"

"Sorry, Joe, but I just like to needle him bit." Dave chuckled.

Slowly they drove down the mile long road which led to the cabin. Everyone was looking intently for signs of the hunters but no one saw anything out of place. Once they reached the cabin they carefully exited their vehicle and looked around.

"I'll check the vehicle for damage." Joe said as he made his way to Marie's wagon. He looked at the tires but they seemed okay. He saw no damage. "Hey, these tires aren't cut. They look brand new."

Dave and Bill were carefully entering the cabin not sure what to expect. "Ransacked? Does this look ransacked?" Bill asked Dave.

"No, it doesn't. Could Marie have been seeing things?" Dave scratched his head and began to calm. "This looks like a prank. Is Marie pranking us?"

The men looked around but everything seemed to be in place. Puzzled by the descriptions they were given versus what they were seeing. "I guess we need to report this as a prank." Dave said as he turn and left the cabin followed by Bill.

"Joe, how were things outside besides the car?" Dave asked.

"I'm sorry Dave but I can't find any damage to the car or tires. The landscape looks normal as well"

The policemen entered their vehicle and drove slowly away down the long road still looking for ANY signs of intrusion or damage but none were found. Even as they open the gate and left they kept looking for other tire tracks, broken limbs or rustled brush. But NOTHING was seen.

Once they returned to the station they cautiously entered Dan's office. "Hello, men, what did you find? Any arrests?"

They all looked at one another as they removed their caps and sheepishly looked down at the floor. "Sorry, Sir. But we saw no signs of intrusion. The cabin was neat and pristine." Dave announced.

"What about the car tires?" Dan asked as he scratched his head.

"They looked brand new and no flats. No damage to their vehicle sir." Joe spoke as he impishly raised his hand.

"So you're saying my sister made it all up?"

"No, sir, not exactly. We just can't find any evidence that the cabin or property was damaged." Bill replied trying to be diplomatic.

Dan was a bit miffed and confused. His sister has always been honest with him. Why this charade? "Thank you gentlemen. I will take over from here. Back to your normal duties."

Chapter 17: The Restaurant

Marie and Jim walked into the restaurant recommended by her brother. They settled on a booth which was currently away from other customers so they could have a private conversation. It was located on the far left of the front of the establishment and had a large window where they could keep an eye on the police station. As they sat down a waitress came over to take their order.

"Here is a copy of the menu," she said as she lay one in front of each of them. "Could I get you something to drink? I can come back later for the rest of your order."

"Coffee would be nice." Marie responded.

"Same here." Jim echoed as he open the menu. The waitress left and Jim gave Marie a glance, "How hungry are you? It is almost dinnertime."

"I think Daniel plans to have us over for dinner. So I think just a small salad for me."

"Dinner with Dan? Are you sure? What if that is not safe?" Jim looked a bit anxious.

"I think we are safe. After our suspicions, I did my Zen and I am not getting a negative vibe. We can still be careful but it would odd if I did not spend some time with him since it has been quite a few years."

The waitress returned. "Here is your coffee." She said as she served them. "Are you ready to order yet?"

Marie looked up from her menu, "Small salad with oil and vinegar."

Jim pondered for a moment, "I think I want a grilled cheese sandwich, on whole wheat."

"Is that all?"

"Yes" they resounded in unison with a chuckle.

The waitress left as they continued the conversation. "I guess you're right. We don't want to let him know we suspect him. Or rather that I do." Jim gave Marie a wink.

"I guess I need to ask Dan some questions later to see where he is with all this. That might be difficult."

"Marie, you ALWAYS manage to interrogate quite well!" He laughed. "I was a bit cautious of you as well there for a while. Especially when you called me a robot, just like Dr. Morris did."

"But we are not artificial, Jim. You understand that, right?" Marie grasped his hand which was lying on the table. "We are just...." And then she whispered, "Unique genetically."

"Yes, I understand, but it is still amazing to grasp." He whispered back. "It feels unreal. I am a real life super hero! It is every kids dream."

"Well you're not alone. There are many of us. Since 2020 we have been repopulating the earth. I suspect that soon we will be unveiling."

Just then the waitress returned with their meal. After she left they began to enjoy their meal but, since it was getting crowded, they chose not to talk any more while there. They were not ready for an unveiling as yet.

Chapter 18: Back to the Police Station

After having their meal Jim and Marie left the restaurant and made their way back to the police station. Upon arrival, as they entered, Marie's brother Dan left his office to greet them. "Hope you had a nice coffee break. Please come to my office." Dan shook Jim's hand and waved them through the door which he quickly shut. "Please have a seat."

Marie and Jim took their seats in front of Dan's desk anxiously awaiting the news about the cabin. "My men visited the cabin and checked your vehicle and its tires. They could not find ANY signs of intrusion."

Jim and Marie looked at one another with shock. "That can't be, Dan" Marie responded as she turned toward Dan. "I would not have walked here those several miles if I had a car! Also my tires were cut and flat, the cabin was ransacked! And Jim fought 2 men at the gate!"

"That doesn't change the fact that everything is fine now. As a matter of fact, my men said the tires were fine and brand new!"

"Well that's a problem since my tires were at least a year old."

Dan and Marie stared into one another's eyes looking for a hint the either of them seeing a lie in the other. "Then how do we explain this?" Dan asked.

"Perhaps they cleaned it up after I fought the guys at the gate?" Jim interjected. "It took us at least 2 hours to get here. That could be enough time for them to clean up their act."

"Maybe. But it all sounds suspicious to me." Dan replied and paused. "Tell you what. It is late. I'm off duty in an hour so I can use that time to investigate. Why don't we take my cruiser and go to the cabin. You can collect your things, if you wish, and instead of spending the night there you come to my place? We can discuss things there and I can fix some dinner."

"Sounds like a plan." Jim said as he looked at Marie for a response. Marie gave Jim a brief glance. "Okay Dan. We need to catch up anyway. I would feel better if you came back with us to the cabin."

"Great!" Dan arose and grabbed his light jacket and cap and led them to his vehicle. "Jim, can you sit in back? I want Marie next to me so I can catch up a bit."

"Not a problem." Jim entered the rear seat behind Dan and buckled himself in as he closely watched what Dan was doing.

Marie sat next to Dan. After Dan used his thumb print to start the car asking, "Everyone buckled in?"

"So just how did you become chief?" Marie asked with a grin.

"Sheer luck!" he laughed. "After dad died they needed a replacement at the police station. Since dad was chief years ago they thought I might be a chip off the block and asked me if I'd be interested. I never thought I would want the job after knowing what dad went through. But I was thinking about who else they might offer the job and decided that I could do the job after all."

"You know dad would be pleased to know you took it up."

"Yes, which is one of the reasons I did it."

"How come you're not married Dan? I thought you and Nancy were perfect."

"We were. But she died before we could marry."

"I'm so sorry. I had no idea!"

"The FBH just would not let me tell you anything. They have been keeping us apart. They kept claiming you were on duty and could not be reached."

"That really upsets me. I thought they would contact me."

"Could they be worried about you telling me something?"

"They shouldn't be. They have a device in my brain which will explode if I try."

"WHAT! And you allowed that!"

"It was a requirement. Part of the job."

"So how do they monitor it?"

"Are you trying to kill me?" laughed Marie.

"No, just curious." Laughed Dan.

"It is no laughing matter, Dan." Inserted Jim. He was becoming uncomfortable with the line of questioning Dan was using. He feared for Marie. "Marie, did you get permission to tell him?"

"He is a police officer so I can tell him some things."

"Well that is a bit of a relief." Dan sighed but still feeling uncomfortable.

"Marie, do you like your job?" Dan asked as he drove up the hill toward the cabin.

"Yes and no. I like the adventure but I fear the head bomb."

The weather was still cloudy as they drove near the entrance. Dan stopped outside the gate, got out and opened it so they could drive through making sure he closed it once they were inside. They slowly drove down the mile long dirt road toward the cabin looking for signs of intrusion as they went, but none were seen. "This is so weird. I know someone was here." Marie said as she glanced about.

They reached the cabin and got out of the car. Marie walked to her car and checked the tires. They were new. But they were not her tires. "Dan these aren't the brand of tires I bought. They replaced my tires as a cover up."

Jim rushed toward the cabin and hesitated before he opened the door. Upon entering he did not see anything strewn about like it was before. He walked to his bedroom and entered. His things were in place. "Weird" he thought as he glanced around. But then he noticed the drapes were not closed. He remembered they were closed when they left for their trek and when they returned to the ransacked cabin. "So someone did clean it up" he whispered.

Dan, after seeing the shock on Marie's face as she examined her vehicle, realized that she was not lying to him. Then he saw Jim exit the cabin with the same look. "You guys really believe that someone cleaned up the scene."

"My bedroom curtains were closed when I last saw them both before and after the ransacking. They are now open. Someone cleaned up the cabin. But they weren't perfect at it." Jim spoke as he made his way to Dan.

"That does it. You two are coming home with me. It is not safe here right now. Let's load up Marie's car with your stuff and follow me."

"Good idea!" Jim said with relief. He was feeling better about Dan.

They began to pack all the food, clothes, and supplies they brought with them. They did look into the wooden box which held the antique weapons and were surprised that all seemed back. Did they retrieve them from the prey? Or was it them who took the weapons?

Chapter 19: Home Sweet Home

Dan owned a small four acre piece of land where he built his own home. He kept two of the acres as forest where he could hunt for small game and cut wood for heat each season. Fortunately, those woods continued into the hills and mountains and were owned by environmentalists. That increased his opportunity for animals to hunt. He never used his dad's property since it brought back too many bad memories from childhood. Dad was the chief of police but he was also a bit psychotic. He would ramble on about the hunters and seemed to express both joy and fear of the terror they brought into the area. He also wondered if "dad" was one of them.

Jim and Marie did as requested and followed Dan to his home. The house was a small rancher that had an attached garage on one side. They could see a barn across the property near the road which was big enough for a small tractor and other tools. Everything was cuddled on the sides and rear with a forest.

Dan electronically opened his garage door from his car and drove inside. Marie followed and parked in the driveway. "Jim, be careful what and how you ask Dan questions. Try and let me do it."

"Not a problem. You're the investigator and darn good at it!" Jim gave Marie a wink and a nod as he opened his car door exiting onto the driveway. He took a moment to stretch his back and arms waiting for a signal from Marie on their next move.

Marie had left the car and was also stretching her back. The drive wasn't too long but after the stress of the hunters, walking earlier in the day, the police station, the restaurant and the cabin, she was feeling tired and sore. It has been a rather long and tiring day.

Dan opened the door and motioned them toward him. "Come on in! Once we settle on where you will be staying inside, you can bring what you need in."

Smiling they entered the home into a large living room with a fireplace. "Here is the closet for your coats" Dan motioned to the side door off to the left. "You're lucky. I have three bedrooms. Didn't really need them, but thought if I ever chose to sell the place I needed to have them." He again motioned them down a hall and pointed each of them to rooms they could choose. Marie chose the one nearest the living room on the right. Jim took the one across from her. Dan's was at the end of the hall near the bathroom. Dan gave them a short tour of the kitchen/dining area and the deck off the kitchen. "You can bring in your stuff while I start the grill. I thought just hamburgers. Is that alright?" Marie and Jim smiled, nodded, and then left through the front door to retrieve their nightly needs.

Once Jim and Marie finished lugging their stuff they made their way to the deck where Dan was busy cooking. Opening the sliding glass doors they noticed how the yard was positioned. In the middle was a vegetable garden. It was where the sun could reach the plants full force since the trees gave shade to the edges of the yard. "Have a seat." Dan pointed to the table with an umbrella near the grill. "Were your rooms okay?"

"Yes, very nice." Jim said as he sat next to Marie. "You have a lovely home, Dan."

"Thank you. I built it myself....or rather with some help from friends. We helped each other so that we all could afford a home." Dan turned and placed a platter of burgers on the table. "Let's eat!"

As they filled their plates Marie began to plan her conversation. "Excellent burger!" she said as she bit into the meal. "I noticed when we arrived at the cabin that it looked like it had not been used in quite a while. Why haven't you been using it since it is so close? It just seemed to be abandoned."

"Well, I really never liked the place because of dad's stories. They were scary. You know, Marie, don't take this the wrong way, but I sometimes wondered if dad was one of the hunters. He could be a bit freaky sometimes."

"Funny, I thought the same thing but was afraid to mention it to you." She looked into Dan eyes for any tells.

"You asked me earlier why I took the job as chief of police. Part of the reason was I was afraid of who might take dad's place. If he was a hunter, "they", whomever "they" may be, might replace him with another hunter. I just could not take the chance. I know I'm not one. So I took it."

Jim gave Marie a glance, "I'm glad you're the chief. It takes courage to stand up to them."

"There is something else." Dan paused and whispered. "I have a confession to make." Jim and Marie felt a sudden panic coming on. Was he just to tell them they were right? He was a hunter. "I have some hidden talents. I'm only telling you because you're my sister and a FBH agent. And you, Jim, are a client and thus also sworn to secrecy." He then grinned from ear to ear, "I can fly."

Jim and Marie laughed. "So can I with a plane." Jim chuckled.

"No, Jim, I am serious. I will show you." Dan got up went to the edge of the deck. He closed his eyes, raised his arms to his side. Suddenly his body left the deck and hovered above it. "See, I'm not kidding" Dan gazed down at them as he moved about hovering above the deck and then in the yard over his garden. He then returned to the deck and landed. "Well, what do you think?"

They were dumbstruck. "Well, I guess it runs in the family. I talk to nature. And, right now, the birds are a bit worried." Marie laughed.

"You're kidding me? Right?" Dan asked. "I thought I was the only one! I have been keeping this a secret since childhood in fear. I have never told anyone until today. But I just thought I really needed to tell you."

"No. Your no the only one. But your gift is different. Society shuns people who are different because they fear the loss of stability. They normally don't like the unknown. Jim, has a talent as well." She gave Jim a nod. "Show him."

Jim stood, raised his arm and lifted the wheelbarrow into the air and moved it to another spot in the yard. He turned toward Dan. "It was Marie who helped to awaken this in me. It is how I was able to help us escape from the hunters."

Dan was stunned. He sat quietly as he stared at them both. Suddenly he laughed very hard. "Wow! Just how many of us are there? Why are WE? Now what do we do?"

Chapter 20: FBH calls

It has been almost a week since Jim's surgery. Marie was expecting a call regarding Jim's progress and began to plan her story. She needs to hide the talents to the FBH, yet, advise the underground scientists, social economists, and medical field specialists of what the new talents were. Would she have to report her brother?

Meanwhile, she retrieved her computer and visited her reporting site to update, in writing, to the FBH. Her report means different things to the people within the FBH. To the higher-ups in the governments, it means that everything is going their way and control is still theirs and getting stronger. That control gives them the power they want and helps them to manipulate, as well as, increase their finances. Greed and Power are satisfied.

The true scientists, social economists and medical who created the robots to save the world from the corrupt governments run by businessmen who only wanted greed and power, they would see her report as confirmation that their project is succeeding. That robots would inherit the earth and keep the greedy and powerful under check.

Ah, the delicate balance that her reports must convey. But reporting by phone was also dangerous. She had to talk in code to the "true" FBH.

Marie finished summiting her report and began to wait for the code call. As she waited she glanced out the window of her bedroom and was watching Jim and Dan playing in the backyard. They were kicking a ball around and laughing. They were like two little children who became friends by chance. Occasionally Dan would fly up and kick the ball mid-air. Then Jim would catch it with his force and toss it back. They would laugh and joke the entire time. They had no idea of the seriousness of their skills. For now, she just peered through the glass window and smiled. She, too, felt a bit joyful. Being able to share her talent with others gave her a feeling of freedom she had lost for so long.

Suddenly her phone rang. As she reached for the phone, she took a deep breath. Lifting the phone and touching its face, she viewed the image of her "true" FBH boss, Ivy Green.

"Marie, good report on Jim Boggs. I see he is controllable and you have been coaching him on being loyal to the government."

"Yes. He is on board. He is moving along quite well. Much of what he does is uplifting. He lifts my spirits with his support and engages quite well. I feel he is ready to be released."

"Wonderful news. We might be interested in using him within the FBH. Would he be interested in leaving Allied Chemical? We could use his skills to promote the serum."

Feeling a bit stunned, Marie answered, "I really don't know. His mom worked for the FBH, Dr. Ruth Boggs. He might not want to return to them since he spent so much of his childhood with them."

"I see." Ivy pondered a moment. "Well we could really use his skills, especially since he is so loyal to the government."

"Okay. I'll ask him." Marie hesitated for a moment then spoke further. "Jim and I are staying with my brother, Dan, currently and since my brother has been kind to assist us with a place to stay, I was wondering if he might be helpful to the FBH as well. He is the local Chief of Police. He is very uplifting. I would appreciate being able to see him more. Excuse me a moment a fly is bothering me" Marie made a whacking sound with her hand loud enough to be heard on the phone. "So sorry, darn fly was buzzing around."

Ivy knew the code. Marie let her know that her brother could fly. Marie had also told her that Jim could lift and move objects. Ivy was interested in Jim for the underground projects and now adding Dan might also be a plus. She trusted Marie's talent of sensing things though nature. "I will mention Dan to the board. I am sorry you have not been able to visit him due to your work. I will see if we can free you to do that. If we add him as a consultant, he could keep his current job."

"What about Jim? Could he be a consultant and keep his job also? He might prefer that as well. I could then work with them both in your behalf."

"You really like this Jim don't you?" Ivy felt the passion in Marie's voice.

"Yes. Is that a problem?"

"No. Actually, it might improve any work we might dispense. You knowing both of them and them knowing you, should improve results. Does Jim and Dan get along?"

"Yes. Quite well." Marie glanced once again out the window watching them playing.

"Okay. I think I might make you three a team if they both agree to come aboard as consultants. Our government should be pleased to have them promote their goals."

"Thank you. I will discuss it with them and email their response."

The conversation ended. Marie was very happy. She could see her brother more often and stay close to Jim if they would agree. She was also very happy that Ivy approved her having feelings for

Jim. That meant she could have a relationship with him and keep her job.

Marie exited her room and made her way to the deck. As she poured her coffee and watched the men her in life playing, she smiled.

Chapter 21: Entrée'

After finishing their game, Jim and Dan walked onto the deck panting but laughing at the same time. "Dan you gave me a good run for my money!"

Dan looked up from the chair he just sat in, "What money? We were playing for money?"

"No, that is just a saying we used as kids." Jim laughed. "If we were playing for money, I probably would have not played!" He then noticed Marie sipping her coffee watching their conversation. "Marie, where were you? We kept waiting for you to join us."

"Me, join you two out there!" Marie pointed to the field where they were playing. "Not a chance!" She then paused. "But I do have some news for the two of you." The "boys" smiled in their little devilish grins anticipating what news she had to share. "I had to file my report to the FBH and then had a cell discussion with my boss Ivy Green. After which she asked me to offer the two of you a position on my team as consultants to work with me. That means, I am your boss but you could keep your current jobs and work with me as needed. Might either of you be interested?"

Both of them lost their smiles and glanced at one another and back at Marie. "How would that work? And what kind of work would we do?" Asked Dan. "I have my career and can't just leave it."

"I had to share both of your skills with Ivy. Each of your skills or rather talents, could help us to keep the rich and powerful in check. You would be helping mankind maintain a balance and keeping the good from turning into bad. As consultants, you would work as needed and the FBH might be able to free you up to do the work as needed as well. You might be able to do the work at the same time you do your normal work. You would make extra money and we could work as a team. I would love that. I would miss you both if I had to give you up for my job." Looking deep in her brothers eyes, she pleaded, "Dan, I lost you for so many years due to my job. I really do not want to lose you once again." She then moved toward Jim, "And you, Jim, have become very important to me." Marie gently took his hand in hers as she gazed into his eyes as well.

Jim felt the warmth of her ambiance flow through him. "I have become rather fond of you as well." There was a slight uncomfortable silence before Jim spoke again. "I guess I'm in. How about you Dan? I would like to keep playing with you as well."

"So you WERE playing with my sister! I thought so!" Dan laughed as he placed his hand over theirs. : "is there an oath? Or are we just in it now!"

They all laughed, hugged and began to make plans on what possibilities might occur.

Chapter22: Evolution

Jim was lying in his bed slowly wakening from his night's sleep. He was so happy that Marie and Dan would be working with him.--especially Marie. Jim knew he was falling in love with her. Her blueish green eyes and blond hair just made him melt. He has learned so much about himself since he has found her. As he was rubbing his eyes and yawning, he slowly and awkwardly sat up in bed turning as he placed his feet on the floor. "Ah, a new day!" he thought reaching for the curtain to peek out at the day. The day was overcast and a bit gloomy. It looked like rain in the forecast. "I need some coffee." Jim moaned as he arose and began to get dressed for the day.

Once dressed, he left his room and made his way to the kitchen where he began to make himself some coffee in the coffee machine. The house was quiet. Jim noticed but shrugged it off as he went to open the front door to retrieve the morning paper. "Odd. No paper. Dan said it is usually here early." he thought as he shut the door. Then he moved toward the back door toward the deck. Looking out onto the deck and into the yard, he stumbled a bit as he opened the sliding glass door. "Why is it so quiet?" Jim began to feel some slight panic as he reentered the house and made his way to the bedrooms. He hesitated when he reached Marie's room, then took a deep breath and knocked gently on the door. "Marie? Are you awake?" No sound. He knocked a bit louder. "Marie? Are you awake" He raised his voice as well. Still no sound. Then he chose to open the door for a peek. Turning the knob slowly, he heard the click of the knob which released the door. Taking a deep breath he slowly, quietly pushed open the door just enough to see if she was in there.

Marie was gone! He began to worry. He rushed to Dan's room, knocking loudly and yelling, "Dan! Are you in there? I can't find Marie. Do you know where she is? Dan!"

Not a sound from Dan's room as well. Jim quickly opened Dan's door to find it empty as well. The panic was getting stronger. "Where are they?" he moaned as he began to open and search every nook and cranny throughout the house. Nowhere was anyone. Jim stood in the living room looking for clues. But none were seen. So he went outside to the deck and yard searching and made his way to the front of the house. There he saw their autos were missing. "Where did they go? Why would they leave without telling me or leaving a note?" Jim brushed his hands through his hair as drops of sweat began to emerge on his face.

"Where they kidnapped? Why was I left behind? What happened?" he whimpered as he slowly fell to the ground in grief and fear. "I've got to handle this!" Jim said as he forced himself to stop crying and rubbed away his tears. "Pull it together, Jim" He made his way back to the house and began to pack his backpack with things he thought he needed.

Jim made one more search throughout the house and left a note on the kitchen table that he was looking for them and would be going to the cabin since he suspected someone took them there. Lifting the backpack onto his back, he left the house and began hiking toward the cabin property.

He found it odd that no vehicles were on the road as he paced along. There was once again no sounds heard. No birds, no insects, no wind. Just the thumping of his steps as he went. Feeling rather alone, he began to hum and move the branches to try to make a fake wind sound to try to calm himself. He found himself becoming more agitated.

"Alone once again. Everyone leaving me. Mom left me. Never knew my dad. Found Marie and Dan. Now they left me. Why? What did I do?"

Jim found himself starting to become angry. He was angry at Marie and Dan for leaving him without a note or reason to be found. His childhood fears of being lonely returned and were becoming acute. As his emotions grew, so did his violence. He no longer just moved the trees as he went—he was pulling them from the roots and throwing them high into the air. They would seem to float in the sky and then explode as they crashed onto the ground.

An hour or so later he reached the property where the cabin was hidden about one mile inside. Jim pulled open the brush covered gate and then closed it behind him. His anger was becoming enraged as he walked down the dirt road. Now the trees were exploding as he passed them. He was determined to devastate the people who took his friends away.

Jim stopped once he saw the cabin and began to creep quietly along to surprise the kidnapers. He reached the cabin. But there were no signs of life there as well. No sounds. No birds, insects, no wind. Just his own steps, his own voice, his own panting. In frustration Jim began to yell, "Where are you! Marie! Where are you?" Silence. The earth seemed to be dead of any noise but him.

Suddenly, Jim, enraged beyond belief, began to tear the cabin down with his powers and then using his eyes he set the wood on fire. Soon the entire land seemed to be on fire. Jim was in the center yelling with all his rage.

Then Jim realized what he had done. "Oh, No! What have I done? I need to fix this. I need to repair this. But how can I? If only I could turn back time." He sobbed and dropped to the ground in remorse. Then a glimmer of light seemed to enter his brain. "But what if I could turn back time? Would things really change or would they just be a repeat of the same?" He pondered it awhile. "But what do I have to lose?" he thought for a moment. "Nothing. I could gain Marie back. My life back."

Jim stood, closed his eyes, and imagined his old life. He thought of the first time he saw Marie and how beautiful she was. Then everything went blank.

Chapter 23: Reborn

Pumping and beeping of the medical equipment were heard throughout the room.

"Scalpel", the surgeon said as he was viewing the body before him. Slowly he began to make an incision and then pulled back the tissue. "Oh, My. Do you see what I see?"

The attending physician peered into the body. "Yes, I do." he replied. "I've never seen one before have you?"

"No. Now I have to tell him. That will not be easy."

After the surgery the patient was wheeled into the one of the recovery rooms and attached to monitoring machines and given oxygen.

Nurses, doctors came and went for several hours checking on the patient. But he lay quietly without movement. No one was awaiting the man's status. The room was empty and silent except for the machines.

Later that evening, Jim, the patient, was beginning to awaken. His eye lids fluttered a bit as they opened. His eyesight was blurred at first and he felt the oxygen mask upon his face. As his sight became clearer he also heard the pumping and beeping within the room. "Where am I?" he thought. "How did I get here?" The last thing he remembered was driving his car to work. "Was I in an accident?"

A nurse who was walking past his room suddenly saw that Jim was awake. She stopped and entered the room. "Glad to see you're awake." She reached for the clipboard at the end of the bed and made some notes as she read the readings on the machines. "I will let the doctor know you're awake. He will want to give you an update on your status." The nurse replaced the clipboard, turned and walked out the door.

Jim quietly remained in his bed feeling some discomforting pain, puzzled, tired and sluggish. A Few minutes passed and then his doctor knocked on the entrance. "Hello, Jim, I am Doctor Morris." Once he got Jim's attention, he entered the room and closed the opened door behind him.

The doctor pulled a chair from the far side of the room and placed it next to Jim and then lifted the clipboard from the lower bed and sat in the chair. "Jim, I've been going over your stats and you are doing just fine. You have two broken ribs but they will heal in about 2 months. You had some internal bleeding as well which we corrected in surgery. You should be able to go home. As long as your work is not physical, you can also go back to work."

Jim, moved to remove his mask. "Sorry, Jim. Let me help you. You might need to still have the oxygen so if you feel faint let me know."

"What happened to me?" Jim asked.

"Well, there was a car accident. You were hit by another car which ran a red light. The air bag is what caused the ribs to break. One of the broken ribs caused some internal bleeding which is now corrected. The police are still investigating the accident, so I do not have much to tell you about that. But I did need to inform you of your injuries."

Jim listened as the doctor continued. "As I said we did surgery for some cracked ribs and bleeding. They will heal fine. But there is something else we found. The doctor paused and took a deep breath before he spoke. "Your heart was very weak and pumping slowly. We chose to give you a pacemaker to make sure you would live. We repaired your heart."

"Am I now a robot?" Jim asked as his memories of the past began to return.

"No! Not at all!" laughed the doctor. "You may have to adjust some of your life but should be fine."

Jim was relieved as he began to remember his what he thinks may be his past or a dream and how he reversed time.

Feeling faint from the news and the need for his oxygen mask, Jim motioned for the mask to be returned. The doctor arose replacing the mask on Jim's face. After moving his chair and the clipboard back to its original spot, the doctor left the room closing the door behind him. Jim closed his eyes praying this was an end to his bad dream.

Chapter 24: Reunion

"Hello, my name is Marie Gloss. I'm here to see Jim Boggs."

"Hello. Let me check what room he is in." The greeter entered Jim Boggs into the computer on her desk. "Oh, yes. Room 2020. Are you here to take him home?"

Marie was delighted, "Why, yes. Do I need me to sign some paperwork?"

"Yes, sign here." The greeter passed an electric card for her to sign. After signing, the greeter gave her a key to his room. "Where shall I send the receipt of exit?"

"Just send it here." Marie gave her a business card with her contact information. "You may send it by email."

Marie gazed at the key. "This could be the key to my future." She thought as she entered the elevator to the 20th floor. She just started with the insurance company and this was her first out of the office job.

Once the elevator reached the 20th floor, she exited, looked for signage toward the room 2020. Turning right, she walked slowly down the hallway. The rooms all were enclosed but had large windows to view the patients from the hall. She suspected it made it easier for the staff to check up on them but it gave no privacy to the patients except for the curtains which could be closed.

Reaching the room, Marie saw Jim for the first time lying in his bed. He was rather handsome. "I wonder what his ability to heal is." She thought.

Jim was bored. He was not used to staying in bed for long times and this was making him uncomfortable. "They told me I could leave today but never told me when." murmured Jim. Then he heard a knock on the door. Looking up, he saw once again, Marie, the most beautiful girl with blond medium length locks that curved on her face just enough to bring attention to her blueish green eyes peeking through the opened door.

"Hello, Jim. My name is Marie Gloss. I'm here to take you home."

"Take me home?" Jim was pleased. Just how lucky could he get? Marie was back with him. "Wonderful! I'm so tired of being here!" Jim sat up in his bed overjoyed to be leaving and with Marie once again. Marie went to the small closet across the room, gathered his clothes and shoes and handed them to him.

"Get dressed. I will wait for you in the hall." Marie smiled, turned and left the room shutting the door behind her.

"Wow, not only do I get to go home but I can also spend some time with little beauty." He grinned from ear to ear. "I need to tell her about my dream."

Waiting in the hall, Marie was looking forward to the time she was to spend with Jim. She hoped she could obtain all the needed information. But as she looked at the key. "Could this key be it? The game changer? 2020? Have I finely found the job I want?"

As Marie waited, she soon was approached by a nurse with a wheel chair. "Are you Marie?" she asked.

"Yes."

"Good I'm glad I caught up with you. I need to wheel Jim Boggs out and I have this for you." The nurse handed her a clear plastic bag filled with instructions, medication, and prescriptions. "He should not go back to work for at least a week. He should make a follow-up appointment with Dr. Morris for a checkup and to get the final okay to return to work. His employer will need a signed release from him to return as well."

Just then the door opened and Jim emerged smiling but a bit off balance. "Whoa, Jim, please sit in the wheel chair so I can take you to the exit. "The nurse moved the chair near him and helped him into the chair.

Marie walked next to Jim as the nurse wheeled Jim into the elevator. "So, Marie. That is your name?" Jim asked. Marie nodded. "How are you getting me home? My car, I was told, was in an accident so I will assume it was towed somewhere. I do not know in what condition."

"I will call us a cab and take you home. Also I plan to stay with you for the first week to make sure you are okay. Thus I need to stop at my apartment and gather some clothes." Marie was liking how conveniently the situation lent itself to her needs.

"Staying with me? How did I get so lucky?" Jim asked. "Who do you work for?"

Thinking quickly she responded, "I work for your insurance company who helps those injured and need help after they leave the hospital. The coverage in your insurance was added in 2020"

"Marie, I have a long story to tell you. I think it was a dream. By any chance, do have a brother named Dan?"

"Why Yes! How did you know?" Marie smiled with surprise.

"Marie, I think I love you. Can we go on a date?"

Laughing, amused, flattered, and surprised, Marie responded, "Yes, we can go on a date. I'm free Saturday October 10th."

About the author.

Donna Sako was raised in Wheeling, West Virginia and is currently living in Taneytown, Maryland. She earned her Bachelor of Arts Board of Regents Degree in 1976 from West Liberty State College which is now West Liberty University. Her studies included Social Science Comprehensive, Home Economics and Law. In 2001 she retired from Verizon Communications. She owned and operated Alpha Research, Inc. and served as Executive Director of the Taneytown Chamber of Commerce. During her working career she also served as a Customer Service Representative, Small Business Counselor, Consultant, Teacher, and Competitive Intelligence Specialist.

www.ingramcontent.com/pod-product-compliance
Lightning Source LLC
Chambersburg PA
CBHW021056130626
46552CB00005B/2125